TOUCH AND GO

Also by Eugene Stein: STRAITJACKET & TIE

TOUCH AND GO

STORIES

EUGENE STEIN

Rob Weisbach Books
William Morrow and Company, Inc. New York

Although this book makes reference to actual people and events, they are depicted solely in a fictional context.

Published by Rob Weisbach Books
An Imprint of William Morrow and Company, Inc.
1350 Avenue of the Americas, New York, N.Y. 10019

The author is grateful to the editors of the following publications in which these stories first appeared, some in slightly different form:
Evergreen Chronicles: *"Broken Mathematics"*
Harper's *and* Michigan Quarterly Review: *"Buster Keaton Gets Faxed"*
The Iowa Review: *"The Triumph of the Prague Workers' Councils"*
L.A. Weekly: *"Dream of Life"*
North American Review: *"Mom's Diner"* and *"One City"*

It is the policy of William Morrow and Company, Inc., and its imprints and affiliates, recognizing the importance of preserving what has been written, to print the books we publish on acid-free paper, and we exert our best efforts to that end.

Library of Congress Cataloging-in-Publication Data

Stein, Eugene.
    Touch and go : stories / Eugene Stein.
        p.   cm.
    ISBN 0-688-15042-X
    I. Title.
    PS3569.T3653T68   1997
    813'.54—DC21   96-52569
                                                         CIP

Printed in the United States of America

First Edition

1   2   3   4   5   6   7   8   9   10

BOOK DESIGN BY LEAH S. CARLSON

for MY PARENTS

CONTENTS

"What is love?" I asked.

She drew me closer to her and said, "It is here," pointing to my heart, whose beats I was conscious of for the first time. Her words puzzled me very much because I did not then understand anything unless I touched it.

—HELEN KELLER

MOM'S DINER

At Mom's Diner, you tip because you want to, not because you have to. At Mom's Diner, smokers are infallibly courteous to nonsmokers. At Mom's Diner, Shorty the cook always makes a really good rice pudding.

Mom's Diner is right off Allen Ginsberg Boulevard, where Pablo Neruda Street crosses Charles Fourier Avenue. Betty, the waitress, works hard, but manages to put money aside each week for her son's college fund. Betty swears she's going to lose ten pounds and curses her hair for turning gray faster than she can rinse it, but she's quick with a joke for the customers and always has a positive outlook on life. She's done wonders raising Buddy Junior by herself, ever since the tornado took Buddy Senior.

That's her son over there—the busboy with dirty-blond hair and sparkling blue eyes. Clearing the tables, grinning at the customers, or baby-sitting Shorty's daughter in the basement, Buddy always has a positive outlook on life. What a charming young man: seventeen, handsome, with a slight gap between his teeth that makes his smile look mischievous. And he does enjoy pulling pranks on young children.

Buddy works at the restaurant in the evenings, but he also plays in the school band and on the football team. You should see him at football games: he slips out of his shoulder pads at halftime, puts on a band uniform, grabs his trombone, and joins the brass section for a swinging version of "The Night the Lights Went Out in Georgia." No one knows about his hearing loss, suffered in an obscure boating accident; he reads lips in the huddle. (By the way, what was he really doing with little Stevie Woodmere on Cather Island? Did they find the buried treasure? Was the ghost no ghost at all, but rather Mr. Parkinson dressed in a white sheet, trying to scare off any thrill-seekers and protect his valuable uranium deposits?)

Then, too, no one knows about Buddy's private tragedy: not his father's death, or rather not only; no, we're speaking of his blind desires, his passion, his deceit. Shhh.

Oh, now he's flirting nervously with Sally, the pretty sixteen-year-old at the counter—the one who's drinking a cherry cola through a straw. With her straight red hair, her puppy-dog brown eyes, and her freckles, she looks so provocative and yet so girl-next-doorish. Sigh. She doesn't even know she's pretty! Sally wants to be a veterinarian, because she loves animals. It's very hard to be a veterinarian, she realizes; you need good grades, so she studies very hard. But with her positive outlook on life, and her flair for calculus, physics, organic chemistry, anatomy, and animal husbandry, she's a shoo-in, don't you think?

At Mom's Diner, gays and lesbians are allowed to serve in the military.

Sally leaves, but look who's coming in: two regulars, Larraine and Nikolai. Larraine is an African-American woman, proud, well-spoken, but somewhat brittle. She'd rather not talk about her past, Betty has noticed. Larraine works as a teller in the bank down the street. The vice-president wouldn't know what to do without her, and in fact, she taught him his job. Larraine and Shorty have a combative relationship, and constantly skewer each other with jibes that display their brilliant comic timing.

Nikolai is an immigrant from Russia. He works twelve hours a day slaughtering chickens in a filthy abattoir. He drinks too much, is accident-prone, and has already chopped a finger off with a meat cleaver, but his mangled English is a constant source of amusement to the patrons of Mom's Diner. Larraine and Nikolai don't have many friends in town, but with their positive outlooks on life, they're sure to fit in eventually.

Now who's this entering the diner? He doesn't look familiar. His eyes are glassy, his hair is greasy. He says his name is Dwight, and he takes out a gun. His arm is trembling. He wants all the cash. Shorty says everyone should stay calm, and he sends Buddy and his daughter Samantha down to the basement. Then Shorty takes out his own gun. "Go ahead," Shorty says. "You can shoot first." But Dwight can't do it. He drops his gun and collapses onto one of the stools at the counter.

Dwight confides that he needs a kidney transplant. The glassy eyes are a result of a chemical imbalance. A lack of proper grooming explains the greasy hair. Kidney transplants and conditioning shampoos are expensive, so what else can he do?

First of all, Betty declares, he needs a positive outlook on life. He can start working at Mom's Diner to make some extra cash—Buddy's leaving for college in the fall, anyway. And they'll all chip in for the transplant.

Then Larraine admits, shyly, that she has an extra kidney. That's right, she has three. Betty is sure Larraine and Dwight will be genetically compatible. The necessary arrangements are made. This exchange of body parts, crossing racial lines, moves everyone, even Shorty. Shorty volunteers to give the kid a haircut, but his offhandedness doesn't fool anybody. Deep down, Shorty's a softy.

Samantha comes running up from the basement, crying hysterically. Buddy follows her into the diner. She seems fearful of Buddy. But Buddy explains that to distract Samantha, he pretended his hand was a mouse, and then let the mouse crawl up her dress. Everybody has a good laugh, including Dwight, who now has a positive outlook on life. Shorty puts away his gun. Somehow it's the next morning, and he starts frying some eggs and preparing a huge batch of pancakes. No one worries about cholesterol.

By the way, Shorty's revolver is registered with the local police department, because Mom's Diner has very strict handgun control laws.

CLOSE CALLS

I started taking pills the week my best friend died of pneumonia. I had a bad cold myself and my ears were so badly stuffed I could hardly hear, but I had to fly to New York to attend Richard's funeral. Dr. Vogel gave me something to unclog my ears. The pills made me feel speedy, and I couldn't sleep, so I started taking sleeping pills— Halcion. The Halcion gave me headaches when I woke up in the morning, and the headaches wouldn't go away unless I took Tylenol 3. Tylenol 3, with codeine, was my ambrosia. Soon I was taking codeine every day, too.

And even when I got back to L.A., I was still depressed about Rich, and I still couldn't sleep. I kept on taking the Halcion. Some nights I took quaaludes, which worked even better.

Shula, who works at a drugs-and-alcohol hotline, keeps warning me about quaaludes. ''They go down too easy,'' she says. They do go down easy. You can still get them in Mexico.

Shula is forty-two, divorced, with two kids in college. She's started dating her ex-husband, who works in insurance. I know a lot about her. We talk about once or twice a week. Sometimes when I wake up in the middle of the night and take another pill, I'm not sure how it will mix with the pills I've already taken. Shula lets me know if I need to go to a hospital or anything. I haven't had to get my stomach pumped yet. "Keep this up, and you will," Shula keeps saying. She works the night shift Tuesdays, Wednesdays, and Thursdays, so I try to limit my most adventurous drug-taking to the middle of the week. Shula thinks I've got a drug problem. I do, too. I just can't take care of it right now.

We're in the middle of pitch season—pitching ideas for sitcoms to the networks. There are no good ideas and there are no bad ideas, my boss tells me, there are just good pitches and bad pitches.

Yesterday we pitched an idea about a black rabbi to Fox. We called it "Go Down, Moses." "They love high-concept," my boss assured me. I was mortified. I always get nervous when we go over to the network, but this time I was dreading it even more than usual. I took a Xanax, and then I almost nodded out during the meeting.

I told my friend Todd Levinson about "Go Down, Moses," but he didn't believe me at first. Todd works in research and is very innocent.

———

Sometimes when I can't sleep—and I can't sleep most of the time—I walk down Fairfax Avenue. My father lived here right after the war, right in this same neighborhood, right off Fairfax. Now, at night, the homeless people congregate here. The stores are closed, and the old-age homes are quiet, and even the hotels on Beverly don't seem to be doing much business.

I get the feeling these streets are haunted. Maybe it's the quiet, or maybe it's thinking that my father walked here, or maybe I'm the one who's haunted. Maybe it's just the drugs.

I walk and I walk and I just wish I could go to sleep. The other night a bum told me, ''You don't look too good.''

I spoke to Richard's mother last week, and she'd just come back from a vacation in England, and she told me that when she got home there was a message on the answering machine—an old friend of Richard's was trying to track him down. That's always the worst part, she said, breaking the news to Rich's friends.

Rich was an only child and I know his mother's lonely. I'm lonely too. He was my best friend for twenty years. It seems such a small, petty thing to say, but I miss having a best friend.

Todd's the only one at the studio I trust. He's just come back from seeing his girlfriend, who lives in San Jose.

"How's Cathy?" I ask him.

He just grins. He wears a goofy smile all day Monday whenever he's seen her for the weekend.

"How you doing?" he asks me, quietly. He's come to my office to visit. He's got a quiet, soft voice, and it's tempting to let him know everything—but usually I keep a little bit back. . . .

"Not too bad."

He waits for more.

"Half a sleeping pill on Friday night because I couldn't unwind," I say. "And Saturday night I did some relaxation exercises and didn't take anything at all." Sure—a relaxation tape and a couple of Valiums and a bottle of cabernet. And two sleeping pills on Friday. "Last night I just took half a Xanax. My doctor says that's okay." Yeah, right. Half a Xanax. "I'm doing fine. Really."

"Good. That's good."

It's almost too easy to fool him. He's a nice guy, a really sweet guy. I've told him about the drugs because I have to tell somebody, and it keeps me a little more honest. Not much—but a little.

"You know, you're going to have to do something eventually," Todd tells me.

"I know. After pitch season, Todd."

"Okay," Todd says.

I call up Shula. Two Halcions. Two Donnatals. Three glasses of wine. Two Darvons.

Shula, excited: "Oh, baby, I'm gonna have to look this one up!"

Shula, laughing: "You're killing yourself, baby. Little by little. You know that, don't you?"

I take Tylenol 3 for my sore throat. I take Darvon for my sore back. I take Donnatal for a nervous stomach. I take Valium or Xanax when I have to speak in front of a large audience. If you really want pills, you can always get them somewhere.

My father had trouble sleeping, too. He was pretty much a drunk, my dad, but I always got along with him. I always fought with my mother, even though she was the sober one. My dad never admitted he had a drinking problem. "If you worked where I work, you'd be drinking too," he told us.

He hated pills. Wouldn't take an aspirin, thought aspirin was for sissies.

He developed pancreatitis, although he denied the drinking had anything to do with it. The pain was so intense he finally started taking the pills the doctors prescribed.

"The pills are killing me," he'd say, washing them down with some Johnnie Walker.

My father's dead, and my best friend's dead, and my brother can't hold down a job, and I was always the one who succeeded, always the one who set goals, always the one who had to do everything perfectly. I take pills perfectly, too. I don't even need water to swallow them.

I'm walking down Fairfax, late at night, and I'm asking myself, half-stoned and bleary-eyed, who is this specter always behind me? Who's this grim companion whispering in my ear, telling me everything I've ever done wrong, reminding me of every mistake I make at the job, laughing at every failed romance, laughing at my future. Laughing.

I pass a homeless man, and I remember what Todd once said: "Whenever I see one of these guys, I always think he must be somebody's brother."

I told him, "I always think he may be *my* brother."

My secretary Helen's on maternity leave for a couple of months and she comes to the office to tell me she won't be coming back. She wants to stay home with her baby. We've become friends over the last two years, and she's worried that I'll be mad at her. I'm not mad at her. I'm jealous.

"You're sure you're okay?" Helen asks me.

"Of course I'm okay."

I start interviewing for a new assistant, and a lot of people want to work in comedy development, and I guess I'm not the worst boss in the world, because two dozen people apply for the job.

At the end of one interview, a woman says to me, "I just want you to know, I'm a sister, and we could help each other."

I'm a sister, she says.

The first thing that goes through my mind is, *she's a nun?*

But I know that's stupid, and then I think: she's telling me she's black? I know she's black.

But that's stupid too. I can't figure out what she means. And then I realize, she's telling me she's gay.

We're at the network and it's our last pitch of the season. My boss, Harold, is getting more and more nervous. We're watching our writers strike out. They're not pitching very well, but that's not the biggest problem. Marshall, the network VP, just doesn't seem to be responding to the material.

The writers are finishing up, and Marshall's beginning

to say he'll get back to us; when Marshall says he'll get back to you, you're dead.

And then, right before the writers get up to leave, I say, "You know, we've talked about another way of going with this."

We've never talked about any other way.

The writers are looking at me—not angrily, hopefully. Harold's looking at me, and praying I know what I'm doing. And Marshall's looking at me, because what I'm doing—repitching in the same meeting—is very unusual.

"The other way to go is to concentrate on the brothers," I tell Marshall.

"Go on," Marshall says.

Now, I know from Helen, my old secretary, who's gotten to know Marshall's secretary because they spent so much time on the phone setting up meetings, that Marshall has a very prickly relationship with his brother. And I know that his brother isn't doing well financially and that Marshall lends him money. It's amazing what Helen can find out. I'm going to miss her.

"Really, what we'd like to explore here is what happens when one brother is affluent, and the other brother isn't. We'd like to examine the issues this raises for their relationship and for their families. Class differences aren't addressed in television, especially not in the half-hour field. Here's a way to be true to those really powerful disparities, but in a funny, warm, upbeat way." I'm really slinging the shit, but Marshall's all ears.

And now the writers are piping in—they see that Marshall's getting excited—and we talk some more, and by the end of the meeting, we've got a script commitment.

"That was great." Harold slaps me on my back.

This is how you can be a junkie and still get a Christmas bonus.

We're spending hours every day breaking stories for the pilot scripts. I've always found this the hardest part of the development season. After we come up with a story that finally works, we still have to pitch it to the network, and the network always makes us change it.

I'm working late at night, and Todd comes to my office.

"How you doing?" he says.

I've been avoiding him, I think. Maybe.

"I'm okay. You?"

"Great, great." He takes the Slinky off my desk and starts playing with it. "All your pitches are done, huh?"

"Yeah, we had a pretty good season."

"You said after pitch season, you'd do something." He's not looking at me. "About your pills."

"Todd, not right now. We're breaking stories. You know how busy we are."

"You said you'd do something after pitch season," he reminds me again.

I don't answer.

"You look like shit," Todd says.

"Fuck you."

He doesn't say anything.

"If I look like shit, how come Harold hasn't said anything to me?"

"Harold wouldn't care if you dropped dead if it meant he got another series ordered."

I can't argue with that.

"Give me a little time," I tell Todd.

And some time goes by . . . and most of the stories have finally been approved, and quite a few writers have already started their scripts.

And I'm still not sleeping very well. I walk down Fairfax, past the Silent Movie Theater, silent at night, and Canter's Deli, barely busy, and the small groceries, with the gates drawn down, and the discount stores, with the shutters shuttered tightly; and I walk east on Beverly, past doughnut shop, restaurant, synagogue, doughnut shop, restaurant, synagogue; and then north on La Brea, with its trendy shops and its bag ladies trundling soda cans.

Specters, all around me. At night, in Los Angeles, the

past seems more alive than the present. During the day, there is no past—not in Los Angeles.

"You still calling, baby?" Shula can't believe it. "I thought you'd be gone by now."

"I'm a tough old bird."

"Not tough enough," Shula says. "I've known tough guys. Tougher than you."

"Yeah?"

"They're dead," Shula says. "Say hi to them for me."

I don't see much of Todd, but when we pass each other in the hall, we smile at each other, and a kind of warmth flows between us; and when we ride the elevator together, just the two of us, we talk about the Mets and the Dodgers, about the Knicks and the Lakers.

And one day I realized Richard had been dead for a year, *a year,* and I went to Todd's office to talk to him, and he was very nice. But he thought Rich and I had been lovers—he didn't understand. . . .

I never take alcohol with quaaludes. I've done some stupid things, but I draw the line at comas.

"You think you're so smart," Shula says. "Well, you don't seem too smart to me. My nephew was smart. He OD'd, nice and quick. This slow dance you're doing, I don't understand it."

"Yes, Shula, it's a slow shitty death waltz."

"Oh, very nice, very poetic. Your mama's gonna bury your white poet ass."

As soon as Todd picks up the Slinky, I know I'm in trouble.

"I hear you got all your scripts in," he tells me.

"Look, before you say anything, I want you to know I've already made some calls."

"Uh huh."

"I've got to stick around until we hand in the second drafts. As soon as the pilot pickups are announced, I'm going to an outpatient center."

"I don't think an outpatient center's going to do the trick," Todd says. "I think you'd better be looking at in-patient."

"Oh, playing hardball, are we?" I'm talking tough, but inside I'm dying. And I know this doesn't make any sense, and I don't let Todd know this, but the fact that he thinks I'm too fucked up to be an outpatient really gets to me. I mean, I don't mind being a drug addict—I just want to be an *outpatient* drug addict. I don't want to go to a hospital.

"How's Cathy?" I ask him. Dry-eyed.

"We broke up—"

"Jeez, I'm sorry," I say.

"Two months ago," Todd finishes.

"Two months? Why didn't you tell me?"

"Because you're a drunk. Because every morning, I can tell you're hungover on sleeping pills. Because you don't even respect yourself, so I'm certainly not going to respect you."

"Spare me your maudlin Betty Ford diatribe."

That's a pretty good sentence.

"Betty got better," Todd says.

A couple of nights later, Todd and I go to a movie. Todd drives. We don't talk about the pills. He walks me back to my building and then up to my apartment, and it seems strange to me that he's coming up to my apartment. And for a second I actually worry that he's going to make a move on me, because I definitely sense that something's weird. I start to unlock the door, but only one of the locks is locked. That's strange, too. I open the door.

Inside my apartment are my mother and Helen and Dr. Vogel.

And I think about the people who aren't here, Rich, and my father, and my brother, who lives in Phoenix the last I heard.

"What's this called again?" I ask them. No one says anything. "Oh come on," I say. "Help me out." I really can't think of the word.

"An intervention," Todd says.

My mother's starting to cry.

"I checked out our health plan," Todd says. "You're entitled to a one-month medical leave. When you get back, they have to give you your job back."

"Aren't you going a little overboard with this friendship business?" I try to say this with just enough edge to cut the kitsch—because I want him to know I really mean what I'm saying, without appearing too vulnerable—but I'm almost crying and I don't think I have quite the effect I intended. "Thank you," I mumble, which seems to work just fine.

"There's a good hospital in Northridge," Dr. Vogel says.

"The Valley? That's too cruel," I tell him lightly, but I'm shaking. A hospital.

"We've got to clean out your apartment," Helen says.

I take out the sleeping pills and the Donnatal from my underwear drawer. And the Valium and the Xanax from my briefcase. And the Tylenol 3 from the medicine cabinet. And a stash of Darvon and Percocet from a small bag I keep in my closet. And the quaaludes, my lovely quaaludes from Mexico, from inside the sleeve of an old Clash LP. And the hash inside a pouch of aluminum foil underneath my mattress. And the Absolut vodka in the freezer. And a bottle of wine from the fridge. And two more bottles of wine from the cabinet over the sink. And the tequila in the cabinet underneath the sink.

And I remember in a novel I once read, a woman takes one last swig of booze before becoming a nun, and I remember there's one last half of a Valium in my travel kit, and I swallow it, and I say, "That's everything." And it's the truth.

And my mother, foolishly, has started to sweep the living-room floor. But you know, I almost understand.

DEATH IN BELIZE

He waited forty minutes for a Batty Brothers or Venus bus to take him from Orange Walk Town to Belize City. It was the cool, dry season but it was still too warm and too wet. He was glad he'd put on sunblock; he burned easily. The Batty bus—an old yellow schoolbus bought secondhand in the States—finally arrived. Greg piled in with his green duffel bags, threw them overhead on the rack beside a couple of chickens cooped in wire cages, and sat awkwardly in a small, low seat next to a window.

The bus driver, a sour Creole, drove like Greg's father—bored, barely paying attention to the road, and yet somehow perfectly. The young American tourists in the back of the bus were terrified. Greg enjoyed the ride.

He had worked for Domino Sugar for three years, helping to supervise sugar processing in Peru. But with the Lima Plague spreading throughout South America, Domino had recently moved much of its operations north to Orange Walk

Town, the center of the sugar industry in Belize. For the past three months Greg had lived in the quiet community, working long hours and weekends. In the evenings he talked to the mestizo merchants in his good but not quite fluent Spanish; if it was still light out, he tossed around a football with two Mennonite teenagers. The boys tried to teach him their dialect, but he learned languages slowly. Several thousand Mennonites had settled in British Honduras in 1958, and now they were the most prosperous farmers in Belize, or at least the most prosperous farmers who didn't grow marijuana. "Dis de fu we chicken" a sign in town proudly proclaimed: "This is our chicken," the Creole slogan of the Mennonite Quality Poultry Products company.

With all the sugar processed, and before he returned home to Chicago, Greg was treating himself to a vacation exploring Belize. The fifty-five-mile bus ride to Belize City took almost two hours. He thought about moving to the back of the bus and talking to the tourists, especially since one of them, a young man, had a round, ripe laugh that sounded to Greg much like his brother's. He turned around to get a better look, but the young man saw him staring, and Greg was too embarrassed to go back and speak to him. When they reached Belize City, he asked the bus driver to drop him off in front of the Fort George Hotel. The driver refused at first to make the extra stop, but Greg gave him two dollars and the Creole complied.

Outside the hotel, a teenaged girl, blond and pale, wearing a bikini top and shorts, and a teenaged boy, whose dark skin gleamed under the harsh sunlight, were kissing hungrily. The boy wore shorts and sandals but no shirt. Lean and muscular, he had the body of a man, although his face was still a boy's.

A well-dressed American woman came out of the hotel. She was in her late thirties, blond, slim, and darkly tanned, but tight-skinned, with a tense mouth and anxious eyes. The boy ran as soon as he saw her. The woman screamed at the girl—her daughter, Greg assumed—grabbed her roughly by the arm, and pulled her into the hotel. The girl started crying.

Greg followed them into the building. He paid too much for his small, plain single but at least had a view of the tin roofs and the turbid canals of Belize City out of one window and a view of the blue harbor out of another. He tipped the bellboy who had brought his duffel bags up to his room and then went down to the bar.

A good-looking Latino man, quite young, was sitting at the bar next to an older, portly British man with a gray mustache. Greg sat at a side table and ordered some food. The elderly gent, wearing a bow tie and carrying a Penguin paperback, asked the bartender for an aspirin. Nodding goodbye to his neighbors at the bar, he tottered out of the room, his round face looking slightly pinched. Greg caught the eye of the young man, looked away, and ordered a beer. The beer was served warm. Greg had carried a book with him into the bar and started to read.

"I think I know you, *señor,* no?"

Greg, surprised, looked up from his book at the good-looking Latino, who had approached his table. "I don't think so."

"Really?" The young man seemed puzzled. "Well, it is not so important. May I sit with you, please?"

"Of course." Greg, confused, put down his book.

"There is no one to talk to. Everyone is . . ." He smiled beautifully at Greg. "More old."

"My name's Greg."

"Jorge."

They shook hands. He was even better looking than Greg had first realized. He had dark, intelligent eyes, high cheekbones, and smooth brown skin marred only by a single chicken pox scar near his nose. Jorge told him that he was on vacation from school, and that his friends had gone to Tikal, a large Mayan ruin in Guatemala. "They have the car. So I am stuck here." He had been in Belize for a week.

"Your English is very good."

"No, it is terrible."

"Where are you from?"

"Peru."

"From Lima?" Greg tried to make the question sound casual.

"No. I come from Callao. Have you ever hear of Callao?"

"I lived there for a few months." When the Lima Plague first broke out, Domino Sugar had moved its South American operations to the Peruvian seaport, just west of the capital. The plague was sexually transmitted, although there had been a few reports of transmission through saliva and even casual contact, and at that time was largely confined to the slums; Domino thought its personnel would be safe in Callao. But within a year the plague spread out from the shantytowns into Lima proper, and then from Lima across Peru, and then from Peru across South America.

"When you live there?" Jorge asked.

"Two years ago."

"Two years ago I am already in Colombia. To Bogotá at the university. I am there four years. I never go back to Peru."

So Jorge was probably safe. He certainly looked healthy. The plague began with the patient coughing up blood, progressed rapidly to fever and diarrhea, and ended a few days later when the lymph nodes under the armpits and in the groin enlarged and finally hemorrhaged. Some people, exposed to the disease, remained immune, although they could become carriers. Usually the plague was fatal.

"Your eyes, they are not brown, and they are not yellow," Jorge said abruptly.

Greg smiled. "Hazel."

"Very hazel. And your hair is nice, I like it, it is very white."

"Blond," Greg corrected.

"Why you come to Belize, Greg?"

"I was working in Orange Walk Town. Now, I'm just doing some sightseeing."

"So we may go together sightseeing."

While talking to Greg, Jorge had taken the white cloth napkin on his side of the table and bunched some of the linen into a small balloon. He placed the napkin ring around the balloon and put his finger under and inside the napkin, working it like a puppet. The napkin was transformed into a small, amiable ghost. Jorge grinned at Greg like an impish child.

Jorge led him on a walking tour of the capital. They crossed the Swing Bridge to get to the south bank of the Haulover Creek, passing through the stalls of the vendors at the Municipal Market. Turtles, tied with rope, dangled upside down while the fierce sun broiled them slowly to death inside their shells. Stacks of vegetables wilted in the heat; stacks of fish gleamed dully with their pearly eyes and dripped fishy-smelling oil drops on the concrete below, like beads of sweat.

They walked up and down Albert Street, first stopping for ice cream at the Bluebird Ice Cream Parlour, stopping again so Greg could get money from one of the cash machines that lined the street, and stopping a third time at Central Park, because Greg wanted to see it, although Jorge said it wasn't very interesting. They finished their ice cream before entering the garden, licking each other's cones so they could combine the vanilla and the mocha almond fudge in their mouths.

The park took up a square block of Belize City. Three or four men stood around listlessly by the gate, under some shade, near a Kentucky Fried Chicken restaurant. They stared at both Greg and Jorge, but mostly at Jorge. Greg asked Jorge if he knew the men. Jorge said he didn't—they were probably hoping to sell drugs to Greg and wondering if he, Jorge, would be the intermediary. They made him nervous, Jorge said, and anyway, there was something else he wanted to show Greg.

"How old are you?" Greg asked as they walked.

"Twenty-two."

"That's good."

"Why?" Jorge laughed. "I am old."

"I'm twenty-seven."

Jorge led Greg down some side streets to one of the residential areas. They crossed a foul-smelling canal and at last came to a street where all the weather-beaten clapboard houses were built on tall, thin stilts. Greg was amazed that the houses didn't topple. Laundry fluttered on lines in front of the homes, a rainbow of blue jeans, yellow T-shirts, and red sweatshirts emblazoned with American logos.

They crossed back over the Swing Bridge and sat on a bench overlooking the harbor. "I'm glad I met you," Greg said. "I've been lonely," he added, and then he blushed.

"You are red."

"My whole family blushes. My brother was even worse than me. He used to turn beet red."

"And why you are lonely?"

"I've just spent three months with no one to talk to. Although some Mennonite kids did teach me a little Low German." He could see Jorge didn't understand. "Never mind."

"My mother speak German," Jorge said.

"Does she live in Peru?"

"She die when I am fifteen. My father has a girlfriend all the time, he marry her one month later. She has two children, my father love them, he give me and my brother nothing. I run away to Bogotá. I never go back to Peru."

Greg took Jorge's hand into his own. "Yes," Jorge said, stroking Greg's hair.

Greg asked Jorge where he was staying, and Jorge told him that he was sleeping in the living room of some friends of friends. "You could stay over in my room," Greg said. "If, if you want."

"Yes."

They walked back to the Fort George together, holding hands when no one was looking. The young American girl was back outside, this time waiting around the corner from the hotel. She smiled nervously at them. A moment later the Creole boy came running up. He kissed the girl, grabbed her, and pulled her away.

Jorge said he'd have to tell his friends that he wasn't going to be spending the night, but promised to return to the hotel soon. Greg went into the Fort George's drugstore to buy soap, shampoo, a package of condoms, toothpaste, and shaving cream. The clerk in the store was black, but the plastic name tag on his white uniform was labeled Ortiz. In the space of a few minutes, while he waited on line, Greg heard the clerk speak English, Spanish, Creole, and even some Indian to a small Yucatecan Mayan boy who wanted candy, but didn't have enough money. Greg gave the boy a quarter; American money was good in Belize. The Indian boy thanked him with a shy, curt "*Gracias,*" and ran out of the store with his Milky Way bar.

———

In the morning, Greg rented a car and Jorge joined him on a trip to Xunantunich. They sped down Cemetery Road, where the burial vaults were built several feet above the soggy ground. The road gave way to the Western Highway. Even this early, it was hot and almost unbearably muggy. Outside, swampland was gradually replaced by scrub palm. The highway rose, and to the south they saw the first outline of the Maya Mountains.

Three hours later, they reached San Ignacio and the village of Succotz. A hand-cranked cable car ferried them across the river to Xunantunich. A short, thin teenaged boy, a Mopan Mayan, led them on a tour of the ruins.

"You look Indian too," Greg told Jorge.

"My father is Indian, *señor*."

"*Señor?*"

Jorge, embarrassed, squeezed his hand. "Why not *señor*?"

Xunantunich was set on a plateau overlooking the Belize River. El Castillo, the tallest pyramid, was over forty yards high. Thick jungle encircled the complex and in some areas was gradually strangling it. In other areas, Mopan farmers had beat the jungle back. Greg and Jorge, sweating, followed the guide to the back of the building and up a steep stone staircase to nearly the top. The jungle, green, humid, and vast, spread beneath them. The boy left them alone while they looked out.

They walked back down to the base of El Castillo, their shirts now plastered to their backs with sweat. The tourist facilities at Xunantunich were primitive: pit toilets and a cistern of rainwater in place of a water fountain. Luckily, Jorge had thought to buy some bottled water from a Lebanese storekeeper back in San Ignacio.

"This was smart of you," Greg noted, taking a swig of water. "Have you ever been here before?"

"I tell you, I am here one week. I am here one day and I know to buy water." He seemed hurt. "You think I lie to you?"

"Sorry," Greg said quickly. "I wasn't thinking."

Jorge, appeased, wanted to see the jungle flowers surrounding the plaza. As they approached, hummingbirds darted nervously away. Greg admired the black orchids, the spidery calliandra, and the lurid orange and red heliconia, whose buds were the shape of tiny macaw beaks. He touched the fuzzy stems of the plants. The pink sap left his fingers sticky, but Jorge dug into his pockets and removed a moist towelette, neatly packaged in its Kentucky Fried Chicken foil. Greg wiped his fingers clean.

Back in San Ignacio, they returned to the Lebanese merchant to buy another bottle of water, but he had sold out. The air in the store was motionless and wet. The storekeeper, eating his dinner, fed scraps to a skinny tan cat that meowed for more. Behind the counter, a postcard of the

Beirut skyline, taped to the wall, was wilting from the humidity.

Jorge fished some change out of his pocket and bought a bottle of Coca-Cola, but Greg didn't like soda. Outside the store, they had passed an older Creole man who was selling orange juice at a small stand. Now Greg stopped in front of the stand. Jorge tried to dissuade him. "It is not safe," he said quietly.

"Bacra wanna juice?" the Creole pitched. "Bes' juice in beautiful Belize."

Greg ordered a glass.

"No, Greg."

The Creole poured a glass from a large ceramic pitcher and offered it to him. "If you drink de Belize juice, you mus' come back."

"You will be sick, Greg."

Greg drank the juice in a single quaff, strangely excited. The juice tasted sweet, not at all overripe or acidic. His lips were sticky.

When they got back to Belize City, it was understood that Jorge would stay over again. First they walked down Regent Street, looking for a place to eat dinner.

"I wish I have money so I can buy dinner," Jorge said.

"It's not important."

"If you come to Bogotá, I will take you everywhere, and you will pay never, not once even."

They were nearing the bottom of Regent Street. The door of the China Village Restaurant was open, sending waves of ginger and garlic wafting into the street.

"It is a good restaurant," Jorge assured him.

Inside the restaurant, at the bar, Greg saw the blond American woman, now wearing pressed white pants and a green silk blouse. She looked up eagerly when they walked in, then, disappointed, looked down at the drink in her hands, jiggling the ice cubes.

"I wonder what she's doing here."

"She waits for the boy," Jorge said confidently.

"The boy?" Greg was surprised. "You think she's going to sleep with the boy?"

"No. She is here to give him money. So he go away."

"She looks young to be the girl's mother, but I guess she takes care of herself."

Jorge stirred a spoon slowly in his glass of iced tea. "I am not always so sure she is the mother."

"What do you mean?"

"Maybe she is the aunt. Or a friend." Jorge shrugged. "Probably she is the mother."

They had already ordered and begun eating when the

Creole boy entered the restaurant. He found the woman at the bar and sat down next to her. She ordered a Coke for him and they began talking quietly to each other.

"How much do you think he'll get? A couple of hundred?"

"No." Jorge dismissed the idea. "He is not worth that much. Maybe fifty."

By the time they'd finished their meal, the woman was sliding an envelope down the bar to the boy. The boy opened the envelope and looked inside. Satisfied, he thanked her, and walked quickly away. Greg and Jorge left before the woman but, dawdling at some stores, arrived at the hotel a few steps behind her. The girl, waiting anxiously in the hotel lobby, seemed confused when she saw Greg and Jorge behind the American woman.

"Where were you?" the girl demanded, still eyeing the two men.

"I was just looking at the shops. Tourist traps, all of them. I didn't buy a thing."

Greg and Jorge passed them and took the elevator up to Greg's room. Jorge wanted to take a shower, and Greg realized he needed to go back downstairs to the drugstore to buy more condoms. In the lobby, he was stopped by the assistant manager, George, a chubby black man who wore a starched white short-sleeve shirt, a cheap blue double-knit tie, and expensive leather shoes.

"Mr. Woodman, I saw the boy you took upstairs."

Greg was nervous. The manager of the hotel knew his boss. "He's my friend."

"I can get you a better boy." George had moved closer and spoke confidentially. "I can get you a younger boy. Very clean."

Greg was angry now. "He's my friend," he said again.

"Yes, guv'nor. He's a nice boy." George backed a step away.

"He's not a boy," Greg said sharply.

"Yes, guv'nor." George looked down at his shoes. "I like your friend. He's very nice."

"I don't want to talk about this anymore."

"Yes, guv'nor."

Greg gave the assistant manager two ten-dollar bills.

"Thank you, guv'nor."

Greg walked into the drugstore. There were no other customers, and he chatted with the clerk for a few minutes. He learned that Ortiz was a Garifuna, or Black Carib. The Garifuna were the descendants of shipwrecked slaves who had escaped to the West Indian islands of Dominica and St. Vincent; there they intermingled with the native Red and Yellow Caribs.

The clerk had a little stand in the drugstore where he sold trinkets and handicrafts his family made. Greg picked up a simple, flat cloth doll with a flat, featureless face. "A *puchinga,*" the clerk told him, explaining that the doll, stuffed with black feathers, was to be buried under the doorstep of an enemy; trouble, disease, death would surely be the result. Many Garifuna practiced obeah, a vodun-like religion characterized by the use of fetishes, amulets, and animal sacrifice.

Greg put the doll down and looked over the reed baskets, masks, wallets, purses, conches, jars of hot pepper sauce, and loaves of coconut and cassava bread. He tapped a small drum that had been carved out of a turtle shell, and finally ended up buying one of the masks, which was carved in the shape of a black howler monkey's face.

The little Indian boy came into the store again, this time wearing a Pittsburgh Pirates T-shirt, and Greg gave him another quarter. "It's late," he told the boy, who didn't understand, but who rewarded Greg with a big smile, revealing his rotting baby teeth.

The next morning, Jorge and Greg decided to go to Ambergris Cay, the largest of the islands off the Belize coast. If they hurried, Greg calculated, they could make the ferry. Although it was still early, the American girl was waiting outside the hotel, wrapping her blond hair nervously around her index finger. She shot a look of pure venom at Greg when she saw him.

"What did I ever do to her?" Greg whispered.

"She hate everyone, so she want to hurt everyone."

"Well, what about you?"

"I am dark and beautiful, like her boyfriend." Jorge laughed.

Greg ignored the girl as they passed her, but she called out to him, "I know what you did."

Greg turned around. "Excuse me?"

She had pulled her hand away from her hair and now she was pointing at him. "You helped her find him." She started to cry. "You faggot. I hope you drop dead."

"Let's go," Greg said.

"This girl is very crazy," Jorge told him while they trotted to the pier off Baron Bliss Promenade. There they joined a small group of passengers climbing up a gangplank. As they neared the bursar, Jorge checked his pockets, and smiled helplessly at his companion. "Greg, I . . ."

"Don't worry about it." Greg treated Jorge to the ferry ride. The bursar gave him the wrong change, but Jorge noticed in time.

"At the university, math is my favorite class," Jorge said.

The *Miss Belize* took an hour and a quarter to reach San Pedro, the main—indeed, the only—town on Ambergris. The water, a limpid turquoise blue, sparkled under the sharp white sunlight, but the beach itself was narrow. Jorge said he had heard of another place, a better place. They took a short boat ride to the Hol Chan Marine Reserve, where Greg rented them snorkeling equipment. The fish were spectacular: yellowtail snapper, green eels, blue-striped grunts, purple shrimp. Greg touched the coral reef with his hand and pain shot through him; the coral had sliced open his finger. Jorge put Greg's finger in his mouth and sucked, and a shiver ran up and down Greg's spine, thrilling him. They swam in to get a Band-Aid before lying back on the beach.

Greg poured sunblock all over himself, wiping the excess grease on Jorge's skin. Then he touched the chicken pox scar on Jorge's face. "How old were you when you had chicken pox?"

"My brother is in school, he is six or seven years old, so I am, I think, four years old."

"Where does your brother live?"

Jorge caressed Greg's arm. "My brother die two years ago in Lima."

"The plague?"

"No," Jorge said. "Cancer. Generalize cancer. His funeral is terrible. My aunts cry, and my father cry, and I cry."

"I'm sorry."

Jorge lay back down on the hot sand. Greg lay on his side, facing Jorge. "My brother died too. Last March."

"Your brother?" Jorge turned to him. He seemed pained by the news.

"My younger brother. Hodgkin's disease. He was

twenty-four. I feel guilty, because those last few years, most of the time I was in Peru.''

"You have to work," Jorge reasoned. "It is your job."

"No." Greg's stomach felt queasy. "I went to Peru to get away from seeing him so sick. I feel guilty about that, too."

"I do not think about the bad things. I put them outside," Jorge waved his hand at the water, "so I do not think about them."

Greg told Jorge that the manager of the hotel knew his boss, so they should be careful walking in, but he needn't have worried. There was a commotion in the hotel—one of the guests had died that afternoon—and they slipped by unnoticed. George, the assistant manager, stepped off the elevator carrying a cardboard box. Inside the box was a pair of linen trousers, two pairs of elegant shoes, a bow tie, and a paperback. George walked into the manager's office with the box.

"Poor guy," Greg said. "I saw him in the bar."

"I see him too. He is old."

Greg had a headache and wanted to buy some Tylenol. He led Jorge into the drugstore and noticed that the doll was gone.

"Who bought the *puchinga*?" Greg asked Ortiz.

"A young American girl," the Garifuna told him,

pleased. "She was crying. I told her the *puchinga* would hurt the bad people who had hurt her. I am very happy I can help her."

After Greg paid for the Tylenol, they took the elevator back to his room. Jorge stood back to back with Greg and looked up at the mirror in the corner of the lift.

"Who's taller?" Greg squinted at the mirror.

"I think we are the same."

"I'm taller," Greg decided.

"A little," Jorge conceded.

They turned around and faced each other. Greg went to kiss Jorge, and Jorge kissed him back, at first a little tentatively. The kiss grew more passionate. The elevator stopped abruptly and they moved away from each other just as the doors opened. The young American girl, who looked miserably unhappy, was waiting on the landing. She glared at Greg again. Jorge laughed and ran down the hall to Greg's room. Greg chased after him.

When he stepped on the mat outside his room, Greg heard a soft crunching sound. He lifted up the mat. Underneath was the *puchinga*. "That little bitch." As he bent over to pick up the doll, his head started pounding. "Well, at least I get to keep it."

"You will keep it?" Jorge grimaced. "Burn it."

"No." Inside the room, Greg placed the *puchinga* on the bureau, next to the monkey mask. "I like it."

Jorge shivered. "I do not like even to look at it."

Jorge went into the bathroom to wash up. Greg's head was still pounding. He wondered if he was getting a migraine. He looked at himself in the mirror over the bureau. His neck was sunburned—he'd missed a spot with his sunblock—but his face looked drawn and white.

"Your headache, is it very bad?" Jorge called from the bathroom.

"Pretty bad. My stomach's bad, too."

"I tell you, you should not drink that orange juice."

"That was yesterday," Greg said. Jorge came back from the bathroom. Greg lay down and patted the bed next to him. "Let's take a nap."

"I can't. Greg, I need to go back to my friends."

Greg sat up. He didn't want Jorge to leave. "You can't stay a little longer?"

"No, señor, I must go."

Greg opened the drawer of the nightstand next to the bed and took out his address book. "Let me get your address in Bogotá."

Jorge, bashful, looked at the ground and spoke softly. "Greg, can you give me please three hundred dollars?"

Greg stood there with the address book in his hand. "What are you talking about?"

"I have been with you three days. So three hundred dollars. I am sorry, señor. I need the money very much."

Greg felt himself blushing. He put the address book back and closed the drawer. He felt so stupid, so preposterously stupid. "I thought we were friends."

"Yes, we are friends. We are very good friends."

"But I bought you things. I bought you dinner."

"Yes, you are a very nice boy. But I need three hundred dollars. I am sorry, *señor,* very sorry."

Greg, now angry, stared coldly at Jorge. "I'll give you a hundred dollars."

"The manager, he does not like trouble."

"A hundred dollars," Greg repeated.

Jorge considered the offer for a moment. "All right, *señor.*"

The negotiation made Greg even angrier. "First you have to do me. You understand?"

"Yes, *señor.*"

"Now."

"*Sí, señor.*"

He knelt in front of Greg. "Not so rough," Greg told him. Greg looked out the window. Outside, it was dusk, and several small figures, men, were opening the Swing Bridge by cranking a drum shaft with long poles. "All right," Greg said at last.

He got five twenty-dollar bills out of his wallet and handed them to Jorge without looking at him. Jorge left the room quickly. Greg ordered room service for dinner; he didn't feel like eating out. He read his book and went to bed early, but sleep was elusive. He felt hot and put the air-conditioning on high, then he started shivering and turned it off altogether. Around 5:00 A.M. light began streaming into the room; Greg pulled the shades tightly shut, but the light still hurt his eyes. Finally Greg, exhausted, stumbled over to the bureau. He felt the *puchinga* was taunting him with its splayed legs and thin, floppy body. He threw it into a drawer, but donned the black howler monkey mask as a kind of eye-shade and curled up in his bed. He slept fitfully for an hour or two. In the morning he started coughing up blood.

BUSTER KEATON GETS FAXED

Buster just stands there while the camera rolls. He's wearing his porkpie hat and he's looking directly into the camera. He must have the saddest eyes in show business. The hat he can take off. The eyes he's pretty much stuck with.

It's, what, 1931 or 1932. Buster's just finished a gag for *The Passionate Plumber*. He's working for MGM now; he no longer directs his films and has lost all artistic control over them. He loathes MGM. He despises his own movies.

The camera's still rolling. It's time for Buster's close-up. Buster looks right into the camera. "You studio people have destroyed my character," he announces. The moment is recorded, on film. He doesn't even seem angry. He seems as impassive as ever.

"Cut!" the director screams.

———

Toshiba buys the MGM library. Victor Friese-Greene, the Oxford-educated president of the North American division of Toshiba Software, digitizes the library and pores over it, late at night, on his home computer. Included in the collection are hundreds of reels of outtakes, salvaged by bemused editors. On one reel, Buster's accusation has been preserved.

"You studio people have destroyed my character," Buster says, looking right at Victor.

"Look at that," Victor says. "Would you get a load of that."

"We can do something with this," Victor says.

· "I think we've got something here," Victor says.

Teams of editors begin working on the Keaton material. The images, now in video form, can be manipulated easily, and the editors are able to cut together a promo for Toshiba's new cable superstation.

"I do," Buster says, in *Free and Easy.*

"Watch," Buster says, in *What! No Beer?*

"Super," Buster says, in *Speak Easily.*

"Station," Buster says, in *Sidewalks of New York.*

"The," Buster says, in *Parlor, Bedroom, and Bath.*

The editing begins.

I do. Watch. Super. Station. The.

Watch. Super. Station. The. I do.

Watch. The. Super. Station. I do.

Buster looks a little peaked. "Watch the Super Station," he says. "I do."

But still . . . "You studio people have destroyed my character." There's something about Buster's slander that haunts Victor.

"See if there's anything you can do," he tells his top editors.

Anything they can do? What can they possibly do?

"See if there's any way you can make it more—optimistic," Victor says.

Optimistic, the editors repeat.

The scene has been shot in one take, in close-up. Buster looks right into the camera. "You studio people have destroyed my character."

The editors huddle. They can't cut away. They'll have to borrow the audio from another scene and lay it over the close-up of Buster. But the words will have to be synchronized with Buster's lips.

It's a challenge, all right.

"You studio people have rejuvenated my character," Buster says. No—"rejuvenated" has too many syllables.

"You studio people have brought joy to my character," Buster says. It's not that bad; "brought joy" and "destroyed" match up fairly well, and prepositions are often elided. Still, they can do better.

"You studio people have deployed my character," Buster says. The synch is great, but the sentence doesn't mean anything.

"I want this to *mean* something," Victor tells the editors.

Victor wants this to *mean* something, the editors tell themselves.

"We've got it!" the editors tell Victor.

"Let's see what you've got," Victor says.

Buster Keaton looks right at the camera—looks right at Victor.

"You studio people have restored my character," Buster says.

"Not bad! Not bad at all!" Victor is delighted. "Play it back."

"You studio people have restored my character," Buster says.

"Again," Victor says.

"You studio people have restored my character," Buster says.

"Terrific," Victor says. "Now let's colorize it."

The video is sent to a computer company near Palo Alto. In a few weeks, the tape is returned to Victor Friese-Greene.

Buster is now in color. His cheeks are rouged. His shirt is yellow. His pants are blue. He looks right into the camera. "You studio people have restored my character."

"There's just one more thing," Victor says.

Yeah?

"He seems so sad," Victor muses. "What can we do about his eyes?"

MIXED SIGNALS

We lived in a large, sunny, rent-controlled apartment in Forest Hills. That spring my mother clung to the apartment the way a drowning man clings to a life preserver. Mornings she looked for work; afternoons she waged unremitting chemical warfare against cockroaches. Through successive treatments of a variety of toxins, my mother had unintentionally created a new species of insecticide-resistant roach. The Centers for Disease Control in Atlanta were apparently interested in her experiments.

My father, meanwhile, was growing depressed about his business and spent more and more time sulking in the living room, where my mother screamed at him in several different languages. My older brother, Ethan, was in college and we already owed two years of tuition to Cornell. The university was threatening to foreclose on my father's company. ''Let them!'' my father prayed.

Gerald Ford was president. There was a recession.

There was inflation. My father owned a small envelope factory in Long Island City that was teetering on the edge of bankruptcy. My mother had lost her job as a systems analyst at Blue Cross.

My younger brother was going out with his first girlfriend. They were both fifteen years old. I was sixteen, I'd never had a girlfriend. Yet I was courteous to them. Everyone marveled at how unresentful I was. I was resentful, all right. In fact, I was plotting against them. I didn't know if I could manage to break them up, but I wanted to interfere, to disrupt their telephone calls, to get between them. It was all muddled in my mind.

My mother was in the kitchen, munching on an English muffin and reading a German novel.

She had been born in the Free State of Danzig in 1930 to a middle-class Jewish family. Her father was Russian, her mother was Polish. She went to a German school. Just before Germany annexed the city, her family emigrated to Argentina. She had come to New York after the war and spoke English with an accent, or so my friends insisted, although I could never hear it myself.

"Your father called," my mother said, wiping some muffin crumbs off her mouth.

"So?" I stole the other half of muffin from my mother's plate and began eating it.

"He says he wants to give the business to Morris."

The doorbell buzzed and my mother went to answer it. Then the telephone in the kitchen rang. It was Allie Jones, Marty's girlfriend.

"Hi, Gordie," she said, and I was already annoyed. I wanted her to call me Gordon. "Is Marty around?"

"He went to a movie with Nick and Jeff." I was lying.

"But we had plans."

"That's too bad." I tried to sound sympathetic. "He must have misunderstood."

"Tell him I called."

"Sure."

"I thought you'd gone to a movie," I told my brother later. "I hope I didn't mess things up for you."

"Gordie, I told you I was just going to the store."

"I guess I didn't hear you. Sorry."

My mother prepared an immense dinner that night, and we ate in the dining room, not the kitchen, and on the good china, not the customary chipped white plates. We were welcoming back my brother Ethan, who had come down from Cornell for spring break and who was accompanied by his roommate, Ted. I had been expelled from Ethan's bed-room, which I had usurped the moment he left for Ithaca, and for a week I'd be sharing a room with Marty again. My father sat quietly, eating little, looking morose. I watched Ted eat. Handsome and affable, he had dark curly hair, green eyes, small ears, a broad chest. He looked almost cherubic, except for those glittering eyes and a white scar over his upper lip which I watched flatten and elongate as he chewed. He had grown up in a suburb of Milwaukee, his parents were Republicans, and he was on the crew team at Cornell. I thought he was the most exotic person I'd ever met.

After dessert, Ted and Ethan left to visit some other friends from Cornell who were in town. Marty and I stayed at the table. "I'm giving up the business," my father said. "I'll just sign it over to Morris. The company can't support two people anymore."

"What'll you do?" I asked him.

"Teach. I'm going to take a couple of education classes."

"It's one thing to want to teach," my mother said. "It's another to give up. You need more efficient management methods, that's all." My mother believed in efficiency with something approaching religious fervor. "It's not your fault. Morris is worthless. You do the best you can, but you can't change him, because he's your brother. Well, he's not my brother. I can change him."

"No one can change Morris," my father said.

"We'll see. I'll start in the morning. I'm going crazy here anyway—with the roaches." My mother waved her hand in the air, from right to left back to right again, hopelessly.

That night, forgetting I'd been displaced, I walked into Ethan's room without bothering to knock. I had wanted my trigonometry book. Side angle side. Angle side angle. Side side side. Inside Ted was undressing.

"Hey, close the door!"

I stayed in the room, closed the door behind me, and watched, fascinated, as Ted pulled on a pair of my brother's pajamas. He had taken off his shirt and I could see his wide, pale chest.

"So what's up, Gordon?"

"Call me Gordie." I walked over to my desk and blindly grabbed some papers lying on it. "Good night."

"Night."

As soon as I got back to Marty's room I realized I'd forgotten to get my trigonometry book. I couldn't do my math homework without it, and since I didn't want to go back to Ethan's room, I decided to cut trig the next day. In the morning, I ate breakfast with Marty and my parents. My mother gulped a cup of coffee before heading to the business in Long Island City. My father started pouring boric acid all along the edges of the linoleum in the kitchen. "It keeps the cockroaches away," he told us.

When I came home from school I found my father in the living room, sifting through City College, New School, NYU, and Columbia catalogs. He'd been collecting them for some time, I realized. He barely looked up when the phone rang. I answered it in the kitchen.

"I'm going to be staying with my dad for a couple of days," Allie said.

I was nosy. "Really? Why?"

"Oh, my mom had to go to a convention in New Orleans. So could you give Marty my dad's number? He has to call me tonight, and my father's unlisted."

"Sure. Just let me get a pencil." I stood still and counted off one-two-three-four. "Okay, I got one. Shoot." I pretended to write down the telephone number.

"Thanks a lot, Gordie."

Gordon, I fumed, silently.

"But Gordie, how could you have lost the number?" Marty wailed.

"One second I had it, the next second it was gone. I've looked everywhere."

"How am I going to get in touch with her?"

"She's staying with her father. Can't you call information?"

"I don't know her father's first name. And I have to talk to Allie tonight. What am I going to do?" My brother sounded miserable, and for a moment I regretted what I'd done. He began hunting in the Queens phone book, among the myriad Joneses, hoping he'd remember Allie's father's name. He looked so tormented, so in love . . . as though a fifteen-year-old could really be in love with a girl. . . .

Allie called that evening. Marty had raced to answer the phone each time it rang, and finally his vigilance was rewarded. Allie must have complained about his failure to call her, for he explained rapidly about my carelessness. He started to laugh. "Hey, Gordie," he called out to me. "Allie says you're *not* to be trusted when it comes to the phone."

"She's right," I told him, a little disappointed.

My mother returned triumphantly from her first day at the envelope factory. "It's a start," she said, "just a start. I got Roberts to pay, Hirsch to pay, and Rodriguez to pay."

"You got Rodriguez to pay?" My father couldn't believe

it. He was rinsing off chicken in the sink. He found some liver wrapped in paper inside the chicken, looked at the brown meat suspiciously, then threw it in the garbage.

"Rodriguez?" I couldn't believe it either. Rodriguez was famous for not paying. "How?"

"I wept consistently, and with dignity, like an Argentine. But the overhead on that place! We've got to cut down on our overhead. Morris and I are going to have a talk tomorrow."

My brother Ethan asked me if I wanted to go to Manhattan with Ted and him to see some old screwball comedies at the Thalia movie theater. I accepted gladly, amazed by this turn of events. My older brother never invited me anywhere. Later he told me that it was Ted's idea to ask me.

I watched Ted as much as I watched the movies. When he laughed, his whole body moved, and the vibrations climbed from the soles of my feet up to my legs and thighs. I liked feeling the vibrations. Ted's mouth opened slightly when he smiled and his teeth gleamed. He was wearing my brother's gray sweatshirt. I wondered if he thought I was handsome. I wasn't, but maybe he thought I was.

"Did you like the movies?" Ethan asked me afterwards. We were eating Big Macs and french fries in a McDonald's on Broadway.

"A lot."

"But you hardly laughed," Ted said. "You're a strange kid. Like your brother." His mouth puckered into a wry smile. "You look like him, too."

But Ethan has a girlfriend, I thought. At Cornell.

My father called up a friend at the Board of Ed and just two days later began working as a substitute teacher for a school district in Brooklyn. Unfortunately, the work wasn't regular. "Maybe I could work a few days a week at the business," my father proposed. "Until I get a full-time job. They're laying off teachers but they still need people who can teach math."

My mother shook her head no.

"Just a few hours a day . . ."

"I want you to work there full-time," my mother said. "It's not efficient if you work there part-time. You'll have to pay just as much for the subways and for lunch, but you won't get half as much accomplished. And if you work there part-time, Fran will want to work there part-time, too. And that's where I put my foot down, with Fran."

Fran was my Uncle Morris's wife. Ethan and Ted swept through the kitchen and grabbed two bagels, on their way to the living room, presumably to watch TV. I was torn between my perpetual desire to eavesdrop on my parents' conversations and an overwhelming urge to join my brother and his friend.

"I'm saving your company, you should be happy," my mother told my father.

"Oh, I'm very happy," my father said sarcastically. He dusted the room with roach spray. "Look at the size of that one," he muttered as a roach scuttled behind the refrigerator.

I wavered at the kitchen door—I heard Ted laugh in the living room—I left the kitchen.

My brother and Ted were sitting on the couch, watching an episode of *Get Smart*. I watched the show, and Ted, and suddenly I wanted to touch Ted, I almost reached over before I could stop myself.

"If Allie calls, tell her I'll be there late," Marty told me on his way out the door.

"Can do," I said, enraged and trying my best to conceal it. Did it ever occur to him that I had no desire to play switchboard? That I didn't want to arrange his social calendar?

When Allie called I told her Marty wouldn't be able to make it that night at all. I hoped she'd leave before he got there. Marty called her later and found out what I'd said. When he came home, he remarked with icy indifference that I hadn't followed his directions. I shrugged and said I must have misheard him. Marty's indifference slipped away; his voice grew more strident. "I don't believe you," he said, moving toward me, clenching his fists tightly. If he hit me, I'd hit him back, I decided. He was growing, but I could still take him.

There were too many slipups, Marty continued, he knew I was trying to sabotage him. He said I was jealous because he was going out with someone and I wasn't. Oh yes, that was it, I said with what I hoped was infinite scorn. Or maybe I was jealous because he liked to go out with girls and I didn't. I didn't seem interested in girls at all, Marty said. I was weird, Marty said. That was probably true, I agreed, as calmly as possible.

"Don't take your problems out on me," Marty shouted. "You hate me, and I've never done anything to you."

By now my parents had gathered in the living room to find out why Marty was yelling. I admitted nothing.

I thought: hoboes communicate by a system of chalk signs inscribed on mailboxes, retaining walls, railroad trestles, and underpasses, the signs pointing to food, shelter, police, and so on. I thought: math is my favorite subject.

My father suggested my actions hadn't been premeditated. Rather, I was simply self-absorbed and hadn't even bothered to listen to my brother. My mother took my side. She said it was all a mistake, we had simply gotten our signals crossed, Marty was overreacting.

It was as though I were somewhere else, somewhere far away, the way I felt when I buried myself deep within a math problem. If the answer came out round, it was probably right.

I thought: opposites attract.

"Your brother's an idiot," my mother told my father. We were eating waffles for breakfast. Marty, who had refused to speak to me since the night before, had decided that he alone could destroy the roach colony and was spraying behind the refrigerator. I wanted him to speak to me, but I could not apologize. I could not. "An idiot," my mother repeated.

"Don't say that," my father said.

"You've said worse."

"But don't say that." My father was upset. "It's bad enough when I say it."

"We're just barely staying afloat, and Morris tells me he wants to raise his management fees. Management fees!" My mother's voice rose. "Your brother has a sense of humor."

"I think he's been pretty good about working with you. I'm sure this hasn't been easy for him."

"Nobody can change Uncle Morris," Marty said. He grunted joyfully as he rousted some roaches from their hiding place and sprayed them with insecticide. He sidled past me, unwilling even to ask me to move. My parents hadn't noticed.

"People always need envelopes. We just have to wait out this recession." My mother ate her waffle slowly. "What happened at school yesterday?"

For a moment I thought she was talking to me, then I realized she was talking to my father.

Ethan and my parents were visiting my grandparents. Marty, who still wasn't speaking to me, was out somewhere. Ted was dressing to go out to dinner with a friend of his father's, who might be offering him a summer job in Manhattan. It was my turn to do the dishes, and I had buried my arms in suds when Ted walked into the kitchen. He was barefoot and wearing gym shorts and a pressed white shirt.

"That's an interesting combination," I told him.

"What do you think of this tie?" He draped a blue silk tie around his neck. "Does it go with the shirt?"

"What doesn't go with a white shirt?"

"But do you like the tie?"

"I like it," I said. "But the shirt's boring."

"You're right, it's boring." He took off his shirt. Now he was just wearing the gym shorts. I could see his pink nipples and his broad white chest again, and I could see his white underpants rising over the waistline of his shorts. "I heard about what you did to Marty," Ted told me. "I thought it was a pretty crappy thing to do."

"So?" I said belligerently, raising my eyes, and looking into his eyes and at the scar over his mouth.

Ted laughed. "Not exactly apologetic, are you." He walked out of the kitchen. I watched the movement of his back as he left the room. He came back in the kitchen a few minutes later wearing an unbuttoned blue oxford shirt. "I'm nervous about this dinner."

I didn't know what to say. I was nervous, too.

"Feel my heart." He put his own hand on his chest. "Job interviews scare me. Feel it."

I took a step back. "My hands . . ." I showed my soapy palms to Ted.

Ted offered me a dish towel. I took another step back. "You're teasing me," I blurted.

"I'm flirting with you. There's a difference."

He left the room. Weak-kneed, I sat on one of the kitchen chairs. A roach clambered up the table. I reached for something to kill it with and came up only with a clear plastic cup. I caught the roach inside the cup and watched it run along the circumference, desperate for escape. I heard Ted's footsteps approaching and thought I'd look stupid if he caught me with a roach in a cup, so I lifted the cup and hit the roach with my hand, sending it reeling into space.

"Goodbye," Ted called. "Could you lock the door for me?"

I was a person: I ate like other people, slept like other people, dreamed like other people. I wasn't a freak. I wasn't vermin. I was like other people.

I passed Ethan in the hall later that night. He was talking on the telephone to his girlfriend at Ithaca, who had stayed at Cornell to work on a term paper. "I'll be there tomorrow afternoon," my brother was saying. "I miss you too. Yes, I missed you. No, I missed you more. Yes, I'm sure." Ethan looked at me and rolled his eyes.

I walked to the bedroom I was sharing with Marty. Marty was lying on his stomach on his bed, reading a comic book. He still wasn't talking to me. "Marty, I don't know why I did what I did, but I wish I hadn't done it." Marty didn't stir. "I'm really sorry." Marty continued to ignore me. "Please, Marty, talk to me."

"Oh, it doesn't matter, I'm not seeing Allie anymore." Marty rolled over onto his back and looked straight at me for the first time in two days.

"I can't believe it," I said, caught off-guard.

"I mean, it was never any big deal."

"I screwed things up for you."

"Not really. I just got interested in someone else."

"Oh," I said. "Great. That's great."

"You've kept away from me for a whole day now. I guess I scared you." Ted was packing his things in my brother's room, where I had finally ventured.

"You didn't scare me."

"I scared you all right."

"Well, maybe a little."

"You're a nice kid, Gordie. I like you."

I had to swallow before I could speak. "I like you too."

"Good." Ted folded the blue shirt he'd worn to his dinner and put it in his travel bag. "You can tell Ethan, you know. I mean," he added sheepishly, "not about my little game, I'm embarrassed about that—but about yourself." He folded my brother's sweatshirt slowly and put it into the bag as well. "He's a pretty open person."

"How do you know about me? I don't even know about me."

He had finished packing and was looking at me. He ruffled my hair, as though I were a little boy. "Oh, Gordie, if only you were two years older."

Two years, I thought. In two years I'd be in college.

"Bye, Gordie."

"Bye." I stayed in the room after he left. In two years I'd be eighteen. In the living room my mother was screaming at my father in Polish. Marty was shouting something about the cockroaches. Inside me it was quiet.

The next morning my mother was so cheerful that she was singing, in Spanish. Not only were Marty and I on speaking terms again, but my father had told her that he would give up subbing for the next few months and devote himself to the business. To celebrate, my mother prepared her breakfast specialty, French toast made with challah. Privately, my father told me he'd go back to teaching in September.

"I want to get some ed courses under my belt this summer," my father said when my mother left the room. We were sitting together at the kitchen table. Marty was sleeping late. "I haven't broken the news to your mother yet."

Neither have I, I thought.

My mother came back in and slid more French toast on our plates. "The exterminator's coming Friday. I'm glad things are getting back to normal around here." She eased herself into a chair facing us. "I certainly hope you boys got all that silliness out of your system."

"Well, there's probably more where that came from," I told her.

"There usually is," my father said.

"Everyone speaks in code around here. Have you ever noticed that?" My mother cut off a small triangle of French toast and chewed slowly.

THE TRIUMPH OF THE PRAGUE
WORKERS' COUNCILS

The auction at Sotheby's of European political memorabilia was under way. Jessica Neumann had come to New York from Chicago on the off chance some Situationist material might turn up. Elaine Friedman had come from Northampton for precisely the same reason.

Jessica found herself behind the main auditorium, in front of the long wooden table where the next few lots had been placed before being auctioned. Elaine was already there.

Nothing on the table much interested Jessica—Bolshevik claptrap and reactionary fodder—but on a chair nearby she spotted a pile of broadsides and pamphlets. At the bottom of the pile, she found a single handwritten sheet of paper. She recognized the handwriting at once—it was Guy Debord's; Debord was one of the Situationists' leading ideologues. The document, evidently the rough draft for a communiqué issued during the occupation of the Sorbonne in May 1968, called upon workers to occupy a Renault plant in Lyons.

Inside a large box filled with political buttons, meanwhile, Elaine Friedman had found, tucked all the way at the bottom, a small jewel box with a rusty clasp. She finally managed to open the box and took out a small handmade silver pendant and a delicate silver chain. She opened the pendant. Inside was a tiny painting of Charles Fourier.

Jessica tried to stifle a cry when she saw what Elaine was holding, but a small moan escaped. And then, softly: "Tatiana."

"Yes," Elaine agreed. She turned over the jewel box. A label from a store in Brussels was pasted to the bottom.

"We'll go together," Jessica said.

"Of course."

They recognized each other, for they had both attended a symposium on the Situationists a year before, in Toronto. While the guard was distracted by an old woman who insisted on bringing her Lhasa apso into the auction room—"He has very good taste," the woman maintained—Jessica managed to sneak the Debord manuscript into her program, and Elaine dropped the pendant into her pocket. She left the jewel box but copied down the Brussels address.

———

2. THE PROLETARIAT AS SUBJECT AND AS REPRESENTATION

In 1968, when Jessica was fourteen, she spent the summer with her Uncle René, who lived in Paris. (Her father's family originally came from Alsace, and Jessica had grown up speaking French and German.) A few months earlier, Jessica's cousin Michelle had been one of the students who seized control of the University of Nanterre. The Nanterre occupation had sparked the entire May uprising in France. Michelle gave her younger cousin books to read—Hegel, Marx, Lukács, Benjamin—and patiently worked through them with her; brought her to cafés where dialectical materialism was debated; and accompanied her to a birth control clinic. That summer Jessica slept with a boy for the first time, and she became a Situationist, and somehow the joys of revolution and sexual freedom merged in her mind, so that she couldn't tell where one left off and the other began.

Back in Chicago, her teacher asked her to do a book report, and when Jessica got up in front of the class, she announced that was going to consider the entire Paris rebellion as her text. She proceeded to give a Situationist analysis of the May events. She said that late capitalism really represented the dictatorship of the commodity; that *things* ruled and were young; that modern society as a whole constituted a spectacle, and that the spectacle marked the triumph of the commodity; that by their very contemplation of the spectacle, human beings were controlled, subjugated, made passive, isolated.

When she finished, most of the class just looked at her blankly. In the back of the room, the single black student in the class gave her the black power salute. He hadn't really understood her speech, but he had the sense her heart was in the right place. The teacher hadn't understood what she'd said either and failed her.

A month later she was told she could erase the F if she gave another book report, this time on an actual book. Jessica chose Willa Cather's *The Professor's House.* She said Cather was America's most underrated novelist. She said the characters were beautifully realized. She said the book was a brilliant dissection of alienated labor and the emptiness of bourgeois life, and then she segued into an analysis of the recent invasion of Czechoslovakia by the Russian, Polish, East German, Hungarian, and Bulgarian armies. She explained that the Bolshevism/''communism'' of Eastern Europe was just another form of state capitalism; that modern life was marked by the banality of work and the pauperization of play; that a revolution *of everyday life* was needed. The black student stood up in the back of the room and applauded. This time he got the gist of it. The teacher failed her again.

She was given one last chance to give a book report. Jessica chose *Huckleberry Finn,* and said simply that Huck and

Jim showed how much pleasure awaited us if we could rupture the spectacle of racism and the racism of spectacle.

The teacher was now frightened by Jessica and even more frightened by the student in the back of the room, who she believed might riot at any moment. This time she gave Jessica an A.

3. THE BIG SLEEP

The plane touched down in Brussels during a light drizzle. It was late, so the two women took a cab to a small hotel Jessica knew, ate a light supper of bread and cheese, and then sat in front of the brick fireplace in the common room, nursing their wine. They compared notes: their lives, their lovers, their sense of the mysterious past forever receding . . . And they talked about Tatiana, about her art and her loneliness, and especially about her masterpiece, ''Triumph of the Prague Workers' Councils, 1956/1968.''

Elaine told Jessica that her boyfriend had recently left her for a Trotskyist nymphomaniac, and Jessica shared her pain.

The next day they rose early, ate breakfast, and then went out into the Brussels morning. The sky was as gray as the alley cat who lived behind the hotel and fed on scraps of garbage. Elaine and Jessica walked along the rue du Chêne, past the Manneken-Pis (a fountain of a small boy urinating, and one of Brussels' most important sights). The store, which

71

sold rare books, antiquities, and memorabilia, had just opened when they arrived. The tiny, ancient Flemish owner was still hanging up his coat.

He turned around and looked at them. He spoke in English. "Can I mebbe perhaps to help you?"

"We're interested in the work of Tatiana—" Elaine never even got to finish the sentence.

"Everybuddy want piece of Tatiana," the man told them. "Last week, anudder wooman, rich wooman come."

"There was another woman here?" Jessica asked.

"Yes."

"What did you tell her?" Jessica pressed him.

"I got neckless from old man. Eisenberg. He die. He love Tatiana."

The man went on to say that he had sold the necklace to a European collector who made frequent trips to the U.S., that Eisenberg had a son, and yes, he had the son's address . . . now where had he put it. . . . Eventually he found the slip of paper.

Elaine and Jessica rushed to the address. The son was sitting down to a late breakfast but consented to talk to them. Yes, his father had fallen in love with Tatiana in the sixties. He was an accountant who had done her taxes the year she lived in Paris. No, the pendant was the only gift he'd ever received from her. Yes, he'd heard of the collages. No, he'd never seen them. Yes, another woman had asked him these same questions. She was actually an old client of his father's. The son gave them the address of the woman, who lived in Paris and who had left her card. And they might want to look up another friend of Tatiana's, the son said, a Monsieur Roche, who also lived in Paris, near the Luxembourg Gardens.

They took the bullet train to Paris and were there by lunchtime.

"Tatiana was everything to everybody," said Roche, when they tracked him down. He would have looked dapper in his new gray suit if not for the beads of sweat that had formed above his upper lip. He spoke excellent English. A ceiling fan overhead chopped the air and made vaguely threatening noises, but did little to cool the overheated apartment. The light streaming into Roche's living room filtered through a latticework he said he'd just had built for his orchids and left shadows the shape of a cobweb on the walls of his flat. The orchids were large and almost obscenely suggestive with their gaping mouths. There were packages and shopping bags all over the room; Roche had done a lot of shopping lately. "She could be whatever she wanted or needed to be," he continued. "Her paintings are the same way."

About her collages, Elaine prompted gently.

"You're after the 'Prague,' aren't you?" Roche said.

They were noncommittal.

"Maybe it's better that it's never found," he told them.

"This way it exists for all of us. And no one can take it away."

"Have you ever seen it?" Jessica asked.

"Never."

"He's lying," Jessica said later.

"Hmm," Elaine temporized.

A heavyset man seemed to be following them when they left Roche's apartment, but he disappeared after a few blocks.

Jessica and Elaine went back to their hotel on the rue des Ecoles. That night, they stayed up late, drinking brandy, talking. Jessica said she no longer considered herself a Situationist. In the last few years she had begun reading the works of some twentieth-century Italian ultra-anarchists—anarchists so opposed to authority that they viewed *any* organization as inherently fascistic. Consequently, these anarchists never formed political groups, but recommended instead that individuals attack the state privately and anonymously. It was a lonely sort of life, Jessica conceded, and she felt a certain kinship with Tatiana. Jessica had never settled down anywhere for long and in fact made her living as a court stenographer.

Elaine Friedman was an assistant professor of art history at Smith. She had done her dissertation on Situationist painting, and the work still spoke to her powerfully. She said she felt it was her duty to keep the collages out of museums at all cost, because a museum represented a hierarchical, managerial, bureaucratic approach to art—the antithesis of Tatiana's message.

Jessica went to sleep, but Elaine stayed up late, reading a book on non-Euclidean geometry she'd found in the night table in her hotel room. She went to the bathroom down the hall to brush her teeth before going to bed. She left her room unlocked, since she'd only be gone for a minute or two. When she returned to her room, she noticed that the door was open. Probably the wind, she thought. She went into her room and turned to lock the door. Suddenly she felt a sharp, intense pain in her left temple, as someone smashed something on her head. She dropped to her knees and saw a pair of beautiful blue women's shoes before she sank into unconsciousness.

4. WATCH OUT FOR MANIPULATORS!
WATCH OUT FOR BUREAUCRATS!

Elaine Friedman considered Tatiana one of the most important artists of the century, for Tatiana showed that true art and true revolution could be realized only when art and revolution merged.

Tatiana Basho Malevich was the single member of the Situationist International who lived behind the Iron Curtain. She was born in Leningrad during the Nine Hundred Days siege to an artistic and bohemian family; her father was a great admirer of Japanese haiku, as her middle name attests.

She settled in Moscow as a young woman, and lived there until 1969, when she was placed, against her will, in a psychiatric hospital sixty kilometers outside of Vladivostok. A cousin of Casimir Malevich, the Russian Suprematist painter, she had linked up with the French Situationists when she accompanied an exhibition of Malevich's work that toured Europe. She absorbed much from her cousin's book *World Without Objects,* but grounded his rather ethereal aesthetic philosophy in a rigorous anarcho-Marxist skepticism.

Her fame as an artist rests largely on the half-dozen collages she made in Moscow in 1968 during a single one-month burst of creativity, and which she managed to smuggle out of the country. Distraught over the collapse of the May rebellion in Paris and the brutal repression of the Czechs that August, Tatiana (she preferred to be called by her first name) decided she would rewrite history. She would imagine a world where workers rose up against their overlords, and where revolution was never hijacked by bureaucrats, juntas, Leninists, or spectacle. The six collages in the "Triumph" series were the happy result of Tatiana's reverie.

"Triumph of the Paris Communards, 1871" was a take-off on Goya's "The Burial of the Sardine." But where Goya saw madness in carnival revelers, Tatiana saw freedom. The Situationists had long maintained that true revolution could be seen as festivity, as passionate, spontaneous play. The collage depicts a Commune that has defeated the Prussians. Drunk with joy and liberty, Paris throws itself the biggest party in history. Reds predominate in the collage—the red of blood, the red of wine, the red of revolution. Tatiana gave the work to her father, who lived in Finland, and whom she apparently adored.

The first collage she actually completed was "Triumph of Brook Farm/Fourier Phalanx, 1843," which showed an imagined tableau of Nathaniel Hawthorne, Margaret Fuller, and Albert Brisbane cavorting naked. It is presently in the collection of a Japanese industrialist.

Next she constructed "Triumph of the Peasants/Eternal Council of Mühlhausen, 1525." The collage posited that the uprising of South German peasants led by Thomas Münzer was actually successful. Luther, who had opposed the rebellion and supported the princes, was shown in a stockade. The collage found its way to East Germany, which, from time to time, embraced the Peasant Uprising as an important forerunner to the communist state. Consequently, the collage was shown occasionally at the Museum für Deutsche Geschichte, until an anarchist snuck in and wrote the name "Erich Honecker" on Luther's dunce cap. Twelve weeks went by before any of the curators noticed. Tatiana was delighted, purportedly, when word reached her in Siberia, but the collage was subsequently put back into storage. After the collapse of the German Democratic Republic, the collage was shipped to the Stadtisches Kunstmuseum in Bonn, where a curator declared it "not worthy of exhibition."

Tatiana would probably consider that a compliment, Elaine reasoned.

"Triumph of the Barcelona Anarchists, 1937" showed POUM revelers joyfully hanging Franco, Mussolini, and Stalin by the heels. It was sent to Franco as a birthday present— Tatiana had a wonderful sense of humor—and is presumed to have been destroyed.

Next Tatiana made her most dangerous collage, the one that probably got her sent to Siberia. "Triumph of the Kronstadt Sailors, 1921" showed the seamen tossing Lenin and Trotsky into the Baltic Sea. "All power to the soviets" was stenciled, in Russian, underneath the collage; on top Tatiana wrote (with her blood, some say) "Workers of all Nations, Unite!" Criticizing the Communist Party by invoking Marx— criticizing the Party for not being communist enough—well, it was simply too much of an affront. A day after the collage was first exhibited in Norway, Tatiana was hospitalized. It is undeniable that Tatiana was emotionally disturbed, plagued by visions, occasional hallucinations, and (justifiable?) paranoia; moreover, the events of 1968 had plunged her into a nearly psychotic depression. Still, Brezhnev called her "the most dangerous woman in Moscow" (see Andropov's *Memoirs*), and the political reasons for her hospitalization seem clear. Tatiana's own mental illness simply made it easier for the Kremlin.

The last collage she made, "Triumph of the Prague Workers' Councils, 1956/1968," was actually the most important of all. The "Prague" and "Kronstadt" collages were both thought to be lost when Situationist headquarters in Oslo were set on fire either by Stalinists, neo-Nazis, or careless children. But the "Kronstadt" collage had recently turned up in a stall on the Portobello Road, in London, and Elaine and Jessica believed the "Prague" was extant as well.

5. NOT ANOTHER MOVIE ABOUT TWO WOMEN ON THE ROAD

Madame LaGrange, the woman who'd given her card to Eisenberg's son, had recently come back from New York, her concierge informed them, but was indisposed and wasn't seeing visitors. Jessica and Elaine needed to kill some time. Jessica wanted to see the new Godard film, so she could revile it, and Elaine wanted to go to the Beaubourg museum, which she abhorred. The discussion grew rather heated. Elaine was angry anyway, because Jessica refused to believe someone had attacked her the night before, even though the pendant was now missing. In fact, Jessica started laughing when Elaine mentioned the beautiful pair of shoes.

So Elaine called Jessica a fascist, and Jessica called Elaine a Shelepinite with Nashist tendencies, and they both started crying, and wiped the corners of their eyes with tissues, and started laughing through their tears, and hugged each other very tight. And after that, everything was all right.

" 'Elaine the fair, Elaine the lovable,/Elaine, the lily maid of Astolat,' " Jessica recited.

"My father used to say that," Elaine remembered.

6. ALPHAVILLE, A FILM BY JEAN-LUC GODARD

They saw the special compu-gendarmes everywhere they went in Paris. A small boy used a slingshot against one of the cyber-policemen, then made his escape, swinging from one building to another, using the clotheslines that connected each building to its neighbor and that reminded Jessica of cables linking PCs into a computer network.

"Tarzan versus IBM," Jessica noted.

The sky was as gray as in Brussels, and as the afternoon wore on, the light shortened, until it seemed to Elaine as though the city were being filmed in black-and-white. Or perhaps, perhaps when the light slanted just so and left a pool of shadow lapping up against their feet, it reminded her of one of Goya's dark etchings. Paris, City of Pain.

They walked along the Seine, and it looked like every body of water Jessica had ever seen, dirty, as dirty as Lake Michigan or the Hudson or the Hamburg Hafen. "It's always the same water," Jessica said.

The compu-gendarmes patrolled every street corner, serving their master, Big Memory, as the total computer vector that dominated France had come to be called. The cops arrested anyone who refused to conform; they patrolled against *difference,* which Prime Minister LePen had outlawed.

"Maybe it's best that Tatiana didn't live to see this," Elaine mused.

"What are you talking about? She's still alive," Jessica reminded her.

Elaine was embarrassed. "I forgot." But it was easy to forget. . . . Tatiana had been released only recently from the mental institution that had been her home for more than two decades, and now she lived quietly in Moscow, refusing to see any visitors.

That night Jessica, who was pursuing a master's degree in library science in her spare time, broke into Big Memory's cavernous files with a password she'd bought on the black market in Montparnasse. She managed to find the subfile on Situationist subversives, and by carefully tracking down every mention of the "Prague," she soon established that the collage still existed.

"I knew it," Elaine said. "I knew it!"

In fact, all the evidence indicated the "Prague" was right there in Paris. If only they knew where to look. . . .

A warning light started blinking on the computer Jessica had rented. The compu-gendarmes, probably alerted by an internal security mechanism, were trying to track her down. Jessica turned off the machine before they could trace her.

7. UNTITLED

"Triumph of the Prague Workers' Councils" was Tatiana's most significant work, for it described and invoked— possibly, some mystic anarchist-pagans claimed, it even summoned into being—Situationist utopia: workers/consumers would establish local councils in factories and communes around the world; the nonbureaucratic, participatory councils would confiscate the productive forces of society, and the proletariat as a revolutionary class would thereby seize history.

Authority and hierarchy would simply vanish. Poof . . .

Only a handful of people had ever seen the "Prague" before its disappearance. All vouched for its almost mesmeric appeal; but it was a kind of upside-down mesmerism that challenged passivity, that shattered the spectacle.

Elaine often dreamed of the "Prague." But once it was found, how could she keep it from becoming just another spectacle? "The long-lost 'Prague' "—one more commodity—grist for the capitalist mill. Like the "Kronstadt" collage, set in a little alcove in the National Gallery, garnering quaint praise from *The Tatler* and *Time* . . .

The two women decided to go out on the town. Jessica dressed up in a short denim skirt and blue high heels.

Elaine was horrified. "Your shoes—!"

Jessica looked down at her feet and then back up at Elaine. "You don't really think . . ."

"I don't know what to think. Do you swear? Do you swear you didn't do it?"

"Tell me, Elaine," said Jessica, very gently, "what can women such as we find to swear *on?* On the graves of our mothers, who loved us, but mistreated us, because they mistreated themselves? On the graves of our fathers, who worked too hard for too little money, and whom we can never respect, even though we're moved profoundly by their sacrifice? On the Bible, on the Torah, which we don't believe in? On Marx, who grew old and orthodox and, ultimately, bourgeois with his mathematics? On what, Elaine? On what?"

And Elaine loved Jessica then, loved her because they were very much a pair, because Jessica was the only one who understood what Elaine's life had been all about.

"Swear on the life—not the grave—of Emma Goldman," Elaine told her finally. "And Bessie Smith. Swear on cold ripe peaches on hot August days. Swear on *My Ántonia.*"

"I swear," Jessica said.

"I believe you," Elaine said.

8. THE PLOT THICKENS

Jessica stood there, in the middle of the room, with her gun.

Madame LaGrange sat on her couch, calmly smoking a cigarette and wearing a beautiful blue kimono. Monsieur Roche, next to her, fidgeted nervously. Madame LaGrange's obese chauffeur, Jacques, sat quietly on an easy chair off to the side.

Elaine watched it all, and it seemed to her that she'd watched it all before.

"I suppose you're wondering why I've called you all here," Jessica said.

They were.

"Madame LaGrange went to Belgium as soon as she heard about the pendant," Jessica began. "But the pendant had already been sold. When Madame heard it would be auctioned at Sotheby's, she flew to New York to bid on it. She arranged with a corrupt Sotheby's employee to stash the pendant in a box of worthless buttons, where Elaine chanced upon it."

Madame LaGrange blew a perfect smoke ring into the air, then smiled enigmatically.

"Meanwhile, Madame LaGrange had encouraged the relationship between her chauffeur and Monsieur Roche," Jessica went on.

Monsieur Roche began chewing his nails.

"Relationship?" Elaine asked.

"Of course. They were lovers," Jessica explained. "But Jacques had a secret. Madame LaGrange had slowly and quite deliberately addicted him to heroin. Once he was addicted, he was bound to her forever. In fact, he was her slave. She knew that Monsieur Roche knew more about the collages than he let on, and she knew Jacques would come in handy one day.''

Jacques sat very still on the easy chair. A single tear fell from his left eye and splashed on his cheek. His chauffeur's hat was perched at a rakish angle.

''Madame LaGrange was certain Roche held the key to the 'Prague.' Now was the time to act. Using Jacques as her intermediary, she offered money to Monsieur Roche, a great deal of money, and Monsieur Roche, who had guarded the 'Prague' honorably and courageously for many years, finally broke down. He needed the money for his American cousin's kidney transplant and to pay for Jacques's stay at a drug rehabilitation clinic. With the money in hand, Roche also treated himself to a new suit and the various parcels we saw in his apartment.''

''Don't forget the trellis for my orchids,'' Monsieur Roche reminded them. ''That was very important too.''

''Right. And one more thing. Madame LaGrange knew whoever had the pendant would eventually come to the Brussels store and then to Roche. All she had to do was wait. When we left Monsieur Roche's apartment, Jacques tailed us. He was the heavyset man we saw behind us.''

''I knew he looked familiar,'' Elaine said.

''Madame LaGrange was the woman in the blue shoes who knocked you out, Elaine. At first I didn't believe you,'' Jessica admitted. ''I thought you'd concocted the story so you wouldn't have to share the necklace with me. But when I saw that Madame LaGrange, my evil double, my twin, only wore blue, I realized she was the culprit."

"But why?" Elaine asked, turning from Jessica to Madame LaGrange. "Why?"

"I have my reasons," said Madame LaGrange, quietly but with steely determination.

"She was jealous of Tatiana," Jessica proposed. "At first I thought she wanted the collage for political reasons. Or because she respected Tatiana's artistic vision. Or even as an investment opportunity to hedge against inflation. But now I know it was simply jealousy. Remember Eisenberg?"

"Yes. The old man who died. Tatiana's accountant."

"Accountant?" Madame LaGrange spit out the word. "Perhaps you mean the greatest fiduciary mind of the century."

"Yes, Eisenberg was a genius," Jessica acknowledged. "A master of oil depletion allowances, tax shelters, and depreciation. He raised inventive bookkeeping to an art, and in fact lectured occasionally at the Sorbonne before he retired to Brussels. Madame LaGrange loved him. But he loved Tatiana. Madame never forgave Tatiana. She swore revenge. And what was her revenge? She would deprive the world of Tatiana's work. She wanted the collage, *so she could annihilate it*. And she visited Eisenberg's son, simply to find out if there was anything else of Tatiana's she could destroy."

"That's why you wanted the collage?" Monsieur Roche accused Madame LaGrange, his voice breaking with sorrow, his eyes brimming over with tears. "To ruin something so beautiful? God forgive me."

"It's not too late," Jessica said. "The collage still exists. Madame LaGrange couldn't bring herself to destroy it."

"I wanted to," Madame LaGrange told them, and for the first time a hint of sadness crept into her voice. "I wanted to so badly. But it's very powerful. More powerful than I. . . ."

"Thank God," Monsieur Roche muttered.

"God—or revolutionary Marxism," said Jessica. "You be the judge."

"I have to see it, Jessica, I have to," Elaine begged. "Where is it?"

"Well, I can't be sure—but I suspect it's behind those curtains." Jessica pointed to the blue damask that draped the windows behind Elaine.

9. MARTIAN TIME SLIP

They were alone in the Bois de Boulogne, where the red and yellow irises bloomed, and where the yellow and purple lilies were just beginning to bud.

They were alone with the collage, which was covered with heavy brown paper.

Together they unwrapped it. Together they propped the

collage against a tree. Together they stepped back. Together they looked.

The collage conflated the Budapest Workers' Councils of 1956 and the Prague Spring of 1968; together, Czechoslovakia and Hungary pushed back the Soviet army. The councils were triumphant. The last bureaucrat was hung with the guts of the last capitalist. True socialism reigned.

Jessica took another step back. "My God, it's beautiful. The colors . . ."

"They're *playing*," Elaine said reverently.

In a startling reversal, Tatiana depicted the common people, leisured and happy, gamboling like a court of aristocrats. There were masquerade balls, coquettes, archery contests, jazz ensembles, and in one corner, a Los Angeles beach party and volleyball game.

But the most interesting effect was in the middle of the collage, where a kind of vacancy or telescoping occurred. Tatiana had cut a hole in the canvas and covered it with clear cellophane; and somehow, miraculously, Tatiana had succeeded in bending the space-time continuum, so that through the center, the viewer could peer into another universe. Not metaphorically—*actually*. The other universe was actually visible.

"They talk about rupturing the spectacle," Elaine reflected, "but I never knew they meant it literally."

"I read something somewhere—that anarchism is a kind of miracle," Jessica told her. "The intrusion of another world into this one."

They looked through the cellophane and they saw the other universe. And what they saw was unspeakably beautiful. Unspeakable, because there were no words to describe it. Only mathematics could describe it: anarchism, socialism, freedom, fraternity raised to the infinite power.

But they could not pass through.

10. LIEBESTOD

A wind crept up and swept over them and over the flowers, and then Jessica took out her gun and pointed it at Elaine.

Elaine, nervously: "Jessica, what are you doing?"

"I love you, but I can't trust you."

Elaine was trembling. "Of course you can."

"How can an anarchist trust anyone but herself?" Jessica asked sadly.

"I'd never do anything to hurt the collage," Elaine said. "I'd protect it. I would." She was desperate.

"Anyone can be corrupted. I have to guard the 'Prague.' For future generations. They'll know what to do with it."

"But all we've been through—"

"Exactly. All we've been through. So you'll understand what I have to do. You're the only one who *can* understand."

"Yes, I see," said Elaine, after thinking for a moment.

Jessica fired twice. One bullet went into Elaine's abdomen, the other hit her chest. Elaine fell to the ground. Jessica knelt by her side. And then Elaine took out a pistol. And aimed—

Not at Jessica—

At the collage. She fired six times, and when she stopped firing, there was nothing left. "I had to, Jessica. I couldn't trust you, either. I couldn't let it be put on display somewhere. It's safer this way."

"Yes," Jessica said. "Of course." What courage, she marveled. What commitment.

"The expropriators are expropriated," Elaine said, with a little laugh, but the laughter turned into coughing, and the cough turned into choking.

Jessica took Elaine's hand and kissed it. "I've never loved anyone as much as I love you."

"You swear?" Elaine said, the blood in her throat making her gurgle.

"I swear on the life—not the grave—of Emma Goldman. And Bessie Smith." Jessica kissed Elaine's red lips. "I swear on cold ripe peaches on hot August days. I swear on *My Ántonia*."

"We saw something," said Elaine, content, and then she died.

Note: Any portion of this short story may be reproduced, even without asking permission, even without mentioning the source.

DREAM OF LIFE

1976—See Patti Smith live at the Palladium. Decide to devote myself ceaselessly to her.

June 1977—Patti recognizes me as one of her groupies. She waves to me one day as we pass each other in Washington Square Park.

September 14, 1977—I deliver a package to Patti's mother in Englewood Cliffs, New Jersey. Mrs. Smith offers me a Coke. She tells me Patti is actually a very religious person.

October 1977—I become a very religious person.

November 1978—Hear my first Patti Smith joke on the bus:

Question: What's the difference between Patti Smith and a wet rat playing an electric guitar and reciting poetry?

Answer No. 1: The rat shaves its underarms.

Answer No. 2: The rat uses deodorant.

Answer No. 3: Nothing.

I challenge the young hooligans to a duel. They pummel my body with blows.

May 1980—Patti decides to give it all up, marry, and move to Detroit.

June 1980—I decide to give it all up and go to college.

September 1980 to May 1984—Patti studies the clarinet in Detroit.

September 1980 to May 1984—I study . . . Well, I don't study very much.

June 1984—I interview for a job at Thrifty's Pharmacy. The uncle of Lenny Kaye, Patti's former lead guitarist, works in the drugstore. I decide to take the job.

July 1984 to October 1986—I devote myself ceaselessly to Thrifty's; Mr. Kaye and I grow very close; but after a while, the work begins to get to me.

September 15, 1986—I meet Lenny Kaye at his uncle's thirty-fifth wedding anniversary. Lenny and I discuss Patti. Lenny says Patti enjoys kayaking and macramé.

October 1986—I take up kayaking and macramé.

1988—Patti emerges from her seclusion to release a new album.

1988—I . . . Well, I don't do much of anything in 1988. Basically, I listen to the album.

November 1989—In a newspaper interview (!), Patti says she is growing more politically aware.

December 1989—I vow to become more politically aware.

December 1993—Patti gives a reading of works by Jean Genet, and talks about how much Genet has influenced her.

January 1994 to April 1995—I devote myself ceaselessly to the work of Jean Genet. "Oh go through the walls; if you must, walk on the ledges of roofs, of oceans; cover yourself with light; use menace, use prayer . . . My sleepers will flee toward another America." That sort of thing.

August 1995—The University of Illinois Press publishes my monograph on Jean Genet.

June 1996—After the loss of her husband, brother, and many friends, Patti releases a collection of introspective waltzes, reels, and madrigals.

July 1996—I waltz, reel, and weep.

November 2002—Patti moves back to New York and writes a poem about the Huguenots, using lots of water imagery. It's published in *The New Yorker*.

February 2003—I move back to New York and write a poem about Patti. It's published in *Annals of Preeminent American Female New Wave Singers of the 1970s*.

May 2015—Patti has a grandson.

May 2015—I have a grandson, *completely independently*. (Oh yeah, I got married and had a couple of kids back there.)

February 2025—Our grandsons become great friends.

May 2025—Patti and I meet at a tenth birthday party for our grandsons and talk. Patti has read my Genet book!

April 2028—Patti attends my grandson's bar mitzvah. She sits at my table. During the reception, she sings ''Because the Night'' and a twenty-two-minute-long version of "Radio Ethiopia." Patti tells us, "I used to sing this using feedback. Now I'll sing it using biofeedback." At the end of the reception, she launches into "Piss Factory" and is happy she brought along her vasodilators.

February 2029—Patti tells me she's always wanted to write her autobiography.

October 2036—I finish writing her autobiography. She approves the galleys.

May 23, 2046—Patti dies quietly in Detroit, in her sleep. I miss her so much. . . .

2047—Englewood Cliffs, New Jersey, establishes May 23 as Patti Smith Day. Several other cities and states follow suit.

THE ART OF FALLING

Gus Renfro, an IRS investigator afraid of heights, was about to heave himself out into the open air with a parachute on his back. And he was almost looking forward to his jump. Donny Fortunato had convinced him that he could work through his fear—convinced him over grappa the night before, it was true, but then had stayed by his side during the half-day of lessons that preceded his leap.

Donny was the man whose tax returns Renfro was supposed to be auditing.

Their tense initial meeting in a narrow office behind Donny's downtown store had been followed by a feast of Henry VIII proportions at a Ukrainian restaurant on Second Avenue. After lunch, all afternoon, they drank. Over drinks Renfro reminisced about his ex-wife, a nursery teacher in Washington Heights who, during their divorce proceedings, had built with her Haitian preschoolers a voodoo doll of him using construction paper and Elmer's glue. The men went back to the store for the evening rush and Donny, short-handed, enlisted Renfro to help him scoop the frozen yogurt. The next day they ate beefalo and rollerbladed. They delivered free ice cream to a public school on the Lower East Side and the children, who knew Fortunato well, screamed their approval. Later they umped a Little League game in Central Park between the Harlem Giants and the Beit Jaakov Brooklyn Dodgers.

After fifteen hard years at the IRS, Renfro rested luxuriously on the government's payroll. He avoided his boss and her phone calls. He gambled, ate too much, smoked smelly cigars—Donny's appetites were infectious. Renfro found himself doing things he had never thought imaginable. He picked up a woman who was buying peaches at Fairway, even though he hadn't been introduced to her by a mutual friend, even though he wasn't wearing his lucky jeans. He bought himself an eighty-dollar tie. Now he would sky-dive.

Outside the plane the light was golden. Below him birds flew in lazy figure eights, skating through the air, and the clouds melted, streaming away into nothingness. Renfro looked out the window and realized he was going to die. He had made a terrible mistake.

"Donny," he whispered.

"It's going to be great."

"Donny, I don't think I . . ." Renfro swallowed. "I can't . . ."

An attendant was sliding open a door and Renfro saw a gaping elevator shaft of butterscotch sky. He walked forward slowly and then turned around, his face toward Fortunato, his back toward the open door. His heart was knocking like a quarter in a clothes dryer. His knees buckled. He couldn't stand straight.

"I'll be right there behind you," Donny said gently.

"You promise?"

"Yes."

"You promise."

"*Yes.*"

Renfro fell backward. Donny jumped after him.

Gwen marched into the bullpen. "Has anyone heard from Renfro?"

She had dispatched him downtown, to investigate Forbidden Fruit, a small manufacturer of high-quality frozen yogurt and ice cream. The company was expanding—there were stores already in Boston and Philadelphia, besides the two in Manhattan—but its accounting system was erratic at best. Gwen had ordered a full investigation after the computer spat out the latest Schedule C.

"He says he's still working on that fruit place," her assistant, Hal, told her.

"It's been two weeks already," she complained. "Does he need help?"

"He said no. He sounded—"

"What?"

"Happy," Hal said.

This was perplexing. Renfro was never happy. "All right," Gwen said. "Now I'm worried."

Gwen Hennessey loved Eric Clapton, baseball, and the Gucci handbags she couldn't afford. She was a sweet, pretty, shy Catholic schoolgirl turned tough, hardworking, no-nonsense career woman. She hid her prettiness because pretty women were easy marks and because prettiness could fade. Her mother had faded, worn out by work and Gwen's charming, good-for-nothing father. Her mother was soft; Gwen vowed to be steely. But she wept copiously when Doc Gooden, rehabilitated, pitched a no-hitter. Baseball, and men, could break your heart, even the good games, even the best men.

Gwen was thirty-four. She had thick brown hair, thick eyebrows, pale brown eyes, a narrow chin, a wide, lovely smile (when she smiled). She liked a drink now and then, the stiffer the better. She'd smoke a cigarette, after dinner, if no one was looking. She was lonely, but liked her independence.

She found Renfro in the back kitchen of Forbidden Fruit, eating from a vat of wine-colored slush. "More plum," Renfro was saying to a man standing next to him.

"Hello," Gwen said.

"Hello." The man eagerly scraped some of the slush onto a large spoon—almost a ladle—and forced it on her. "Taste it." He was in his thirties, avid and friendly, not overly tall, and not as lean as the gym rats she saw parading through Manhattan—almost pudgy, in fact. He had splendid tomcat green eyes and wide, pink lips.

Out of politeness, she tasted the concoction. She found a napkin and wiped her mouth.

He was chewing his bottom lip. "Well?"

"What is it?"

"Grape boysenberry plum surprise." He waited. "You don't like it?"

"I don't really like surprises."

They introduced themselves—he was Donny Fortunato, the owner of the small chain of ice cream stores. A stocky self-confidence vibrated voluptuously through him; she didn't scare him, not even with her IRS badge. He wasn't her type at all. Squarish jaws jutted forward from his powerful neck, the neck shadowed by the day's growth of beard. His beard, ginger-colored, was lighter than his short, cropped hair, which narrowed in front to a widow's peak. A thick mat of hair poked through the collar of his polo shirt.

He had fired his accountant and had decided to handle the negotiations himself. She sent Renfro back to the Federal Building, and Donny took her to a Ukrainian restaurant where the bleary-eyed waitresses looked at her suspiciously. After they ordered, she pulled out a folder from her bag and opened it on the table. She showed him his itemized deductions. "Do you have receipts for these expenses?"

He shrugged. "It's a cash business."

"Mr. Fortunato, you can't run a company like that."

"But I do," he said cheerfully. "I spend cash, I deposit cash. At the end of the month I have more in the account than I started with. So I must be doing pretty well."

She told him that he could be forgetting about a balloon payment on a mortgage, or an insurance bill, or he might need some new machinery to make his ice cream. Business could suddenly slacken. "You have no safety net."

"Do you ever smile?" he asked.

He unnerved her. "When I'm amused."

"Put the folder away and let's eat first. We can always do business later."

"Mr. Fortunato, I could close your stores."

He stopped eating. "Oh, don't do that," he said huskily.

———

He told her that he had grown up outside Boston, in Newton. His parents were in the restaurant supply business, his grandparents owned a restaurant, his uncle was a chef, his aunt a caterer. As a boy he rebelled against all of them with his asceticism; he was thin then. The summer after college he went to Europe with friends, and in Italy he discovered gelato. His friends took snapshots of churches, palazzos, Medici torture chambers, Michelangelo sculptures; he ate gelato and gained twenty pounds. Donny had gone through a half-dozen jobs since college, mostly in sales and marketing, but in the end, ice cream was his destiny. If Forbidden Fruit hadn't worked out, he would have opened a bar. "It's all genetics," he claimed. "I'm half Italian and half Irish. I love to eat *and* drink."

She found herself thinking that her mother would like him: he was a Catholic.

Somehow, absurdly, she had agreed to meet him at four-thirty in the morning for his weekly run to Hunts Point Market. Donny had suggested that it might be useful if she watched him do business. He wasn't sure she could get up early enough, but she was waiting in front of her building by ten after four. He drove up in a green Jaguar a few minutes later, annoyed that she had beaten him. "I didn't want you to wait alone," Donny said. "It's not safe."

"I can take care of myself." She opened the low door and sat next to him. "Nice car."

"It's not mine. A friend went out of town and lent it to me."

He drove deftly, thrillingly, through the empty black Manhattan streets, up the East River Drive, across the Triborough to the Bronx, and then along the Bruckner Expressway to the market. Despite the near absence of traffic, he zigzagged around the few cars ahead of him, driving too fast. Gwen wanted to go even faster.

At Hunts Point Donny picked his way through the riot of trucks, drays, pushcarts, and peddlers. Everyone knew him: the trucks honked hello, the restaurateurs waved, the sleepy cops nodded. Gwen admired a baby held by a young mother who was sitting on the back of a truck. The mother let Gwen hold the little girl, and Donny watched her jiggle the baby up and down when she started to fuss. The baby rewarded Gwen with a smile. Donny didn't buy much; he told her that one of his employees made most of the purchases for the New York stores, usually selecting bruised fruit, which was cheaper and perfectly sufficient for ice cream. Discriminating, Donny looked for special items, rare produce or perfect, luscious fruit that called out to him. He stored a carton in the small trunk of the car and asked her to hold a bag of exquisite figs for him in her lap.

"That baby liked you," he said as he started the engine.

On the ride back, he told her how much he loved fruit, how the different bumpy shells hid different beautiful prizes inside. How startling fruit was, with its queer shapes and colors. How had people even discovered that fruit was edible? What genius had peeled the first kiwi, discarded the rough skin, and enjoyed the succulent green pulp?

"I'm allergic to kiwi," Gwen said. "I like strawberries."

He looked over at her and then back at the road. "I think you're missing the point."

A moment later they heard a siren behind them. Gwen wasn't surprised. Donny was driving eighty-five miles an hour.

"Goddamn it." Donny pulled at the wheel sharply, and they skidded off the Bruckner onto an exit.

The tires screamed, but not as loudly as Gwen. "What are you doing!"

"I think the car's hot."

"You're going to get us killed!"

He raced through the Bronx streets, banging the belly of the car on potholes, soaring over low hills, tearing around corners, leaving the cop car behind. He pulled up in front of a subway stop. "Get out."

She tore off her seat belt. "You're insane."

"Bring the figs!" He jumped out of the car, ran to her

side, grabbed her by the arm, and pulled her up the stairs to the elevated, which they had heard approaching. She tried to find a token in her purse. "Jump it," he commanded. They leapt over the turnstiles and ran into the train just as the doors closed. A carful of black and Hispanic faces looked up at them in amazement.

"Well, they can't possibly find us now," Gwen told Donny quietly, furiously. "Look at all the white people with figs. We'll blend right in."

They moved forward a few cars, transferred a few stops later, and then transferred again at 96th Street.

"I'm sorry," he said, "but it's not my fault. It wasn't my car."

"Of course it wasn't your car!" Angry and frightened, she felt herself starting to cry. She didn't want to cry. "You stole it!"

"I didn't steal it. I borrowed it from a friend." Donny wiped her eyes with a clean white handkerchief. "He stole it."

"Ow." Gwen took the handkerchief away from him. "You poked me in the eye."

"Sorry."

Gwen picked up a *Daily News* lying on the seat next to her and tried to ignore him.

"Let me make it up to you," Donny was saying. "Let

me make you dinner tomorrow, and you can finish up the audit, and you'll never have to see me again.''

''No, Mr. Fortunato. We'll do the audit in my office. And I'll bring an armed guard and an attack dog, just to be safe.''

''You're missing out on a great meal. Do you like salmon?''

She did, but she didn't answer.

''I'll make you a personalized ice cream for dessert.''

''I don't care.'' She flipped through the newspaper, and then she weakened. ''Personalized?''

She pored over his file at work. According to her calculations, he owed twenty-seven thousand dollars in back taxes for the past three years, plus interest. Renfro, wearing a new Armani suit, came into her cubicle and handed her a memo, justifying his time away from the office. She glanced at it. He had met for drinks with Donny's suppliers to ascertain their billing policies, confirmed the prices of fruit bought in bulk at Fairway, and thoroughly examined Donny's R&D expenses, accompanying him to a school lunch program, where he tried out new flavors and interviewed dietitians, and to Central Park, where he conducted marketing research surveys with two semiprofessional baseball teams.

"Is that good enough?" asked Renfro.

"It's fine." She handed him back the memo and began to pace. "Mr. Fortunato is a very, well, a very charismatic figure. And a very good salesman. But you never know exactly what he's selling. He has a way of . . . Is that an earring?"

Renfro had pierced his left ear.

"Oh, God." Gwen sat down. "I think we should be more careful in the future."

"What do you mean?"

"Perhaps we'd better interview him as a team."

But she went alone to her dinner with Donny. She wanted to prove that she wasn't afraid of him. She wanted . . . She didn't know what she wanted. He got under her skin.

He lived in a long, narrow, loftlike apartment, with wide, rather old-fashioned furniture. She walked through the rooms while he cooked. The apartment was neat but not fussy. The carpet had been vacuumed, the bookshelves needed dusting. His bed was made. A black-and-white photograph of Reggie Jackson hung over the bed. In the living room, a six-inch model of—she checked the label—a '53 Studebaker Champion Starliner sat proudly on a side table.

"Isn't your friend going to want his car back?" she called to him, eyeing the model. "We left it in the Bronx."

"He can always get another one," Donny answered from the kitchen.

"I guess that's true."

He joined her in the living room, bringing her a glass of wine, a nice white Rhône. "I've never done that before. Borrowed his car. But it was a Jaguar. . . ."

The dinner was superb. The appetizer was blini and black caviar, followed by a carrot and shallot soup. He served a glorious grilled salmon with crisp roasted rosemary potatoes and fresh asparagus sprinkled with lemon juice and a pinch of salt. The salad followed, butter lettuce, luscious tomatoes, and red and yellow peppers, tossed with a light vinaigrette. Then came a selection of cheeses and the beautiful figs he had bought.

"I hope you left room for the ice cream," Donny said.

"Oh my God."

He had made her "Gwen Hennessey Supreme," a strawberry mousse gelato spiked with Hennessy cognac. She was delighted, even touched, by this gift. She ate the ice cream quickly, feeling the tart sweetness slide delectably along her tongue and the roof of her mouth, melt down the sides of her throat, and drip into her belly, where it planted itself, sending quivering cool and warm shoots through the rest of her body. She hadn't known you could get stoned from ice cream.

He watched her eat and he laughed. "Slow down. You'll get a headache."

But she couldn't slow down. The ice cream was too unbelievably delicious.

"Are you trying to get me drunk?" she asked.

"Oh come on, there's not that much cognac." He scooped more ice cream for her. "But yes."

After dinner, she presented him with his tax bill.

"I don't have that kind of cash around." He lowered himself slowly into one of his fat easy chairs. "Not with all the expanding we've been doing. Maybe I can get a loan. . . ." He looked down at the floor and scratched his neck.

"But Mr. Fortunato, I thought your cash system worked so well." She couldn't resist. He looked up at her, hurt by her flippancy, which she now regretted.

"Maybe I can sell one of the stores."

She leafed through the papers in her file. "I see from Mr. Renfro's memo that you delivered some ice cream to a public school."

"What's wrong with that?"

"For testing purposes, Mr. Renfro said. But I find it hard to believe that you were really doing marketing research at P.S. 6. Perhaps your delivery was more in the nature of a charitable contribution."

"You could say that," he said cautiously.

"And I assume these deliveries were regular."

"Very regular. Daily." She stared him down. "Weekly," he admitted.

"Let's increase that deduction." Then she recalculated his depreciation. She waived any interest payments. They settled on fifteen thousand dollars. "I want the check tomorrow," she told him. "Certified."

"You have to have a little faith in people."

"I work for the IRS. Don't ask the impossible."

He sent the check to her by messenger. She wondered if he'd call. . . . She stayed at her desk during lunch, just in case, and the phone rang as she finished her tuna fish sandwich. She grabbed it before Hal could answer. "I want to see you," Donny said.

"Okay."

"I want to make you dinner Saturday night. And Sunday night."

"Okay."

"I want to kiss you."

She laughed. "We'll see."

Donny asked her to a movie, but they decided to go to a night game instead. They took a subway back to the Bronx, to Yankee Stadium, watched batting practice from the bleachers, and kissed as the hot field lights came on.

Gwen looked down at the park with its beautiful, perfect diamond, with its perfect emerald lawn, and she supposed she did have faith. She believed in baseball, in a team climbing in September from the cellar to first place; and she believed in love, with its Cracker Jack surprises. She held Donny's hand. They cheered in the cheap seats, eating footlongs and drinking warm beer, ice cream wrappers stuck to their feet, the yellow moon above them. The game was heading into the middle innings. It could go either way.

BROKEN MATHEMATICS

Even before I learned how to read, I could multiply and divide. When I was in ninth grade, I took calculus and analytic geometry. In tenth grade, I started going to math classes at a college in New Rochelle, down the road from my high school. My principal, who didn't want me leaving the building, put up quite a fight at first; but I have to admit, as soon as my mother began legal proceedings, he became very encouraging. I studied differential equations, combinatorial analysis, and set theory.

Meanwhile, I was failing first-year French. I'd failed once before, so really, this was the second year I was taking first-year French—a mathematical paradox, I pointed out to my teacher, although Madame Gwertz didn't seem interested.

The summer before I started college at Hampshire, my older brother gave me some advice. My father died when I was nine, and my brother, who's ten years older than I am, has always been very protective of me. "Don't let anyone make you take a boring class," he said. "The boring stuff you can always learn on your own."

Last year, when I was a freshman, I had to take mostly requirements. This year, I promised myself I'd take some chances. That's how I ended up in a class on Late Renaissance and Baroque Art. And that's where I met Louis. Louis says I look at the world too logically, and he wants me to throw mathematics out the window, some of the time, anyway. Now remember, I'm the kind of person who sees a seventeenth-century painting by Pieter de Hoogh, "Dutch Interior," and thinks: wow, a Sierpinski carpet (a pathological two-dimensional infinitely nested form).

Simon understands that about me. Simon's the guy I dated before I started dating Louis. Actually, he's the guy I've been dating *while* I've been dating Louis. We're getting closer to the problem.

Half my time is spent keeping Simon and Louis apart. I've never been able to tell Louis about Simon. I want to tell him, but I keep thinking, he'll think I haven't told him before because I don't really care about him, when in fact, the opposite is true: it's because I really do care about him that I haven't told him. I can't tell Simon about Louis for the same reason. And with Simon, it's even worse, because I knew him first.

Simon's a chemistry major. He has to take calculus as one of his requirements and I've been helping him study. He thinks I'm incredible at math. Believe me, I'm not as incredible as he thinks I am. There's a guy here studying complex analysis who can run rings around me. But I have to admit, I'm glad that Simon's impressed by me. I think that's part of why he's attracted to me. If I convinced him that my math ability wasn't anything special, then maybe he'd think I wasn't special.

I like him, a lot. I want him to like me.

I like holding him. He's got a great body. A chemistry major isn't supposed to have thick biceps and funny bumps of muscle on his legs and a flat stomach perfect for demonstrating plane geometry . . . I could go on, but I'd just embarrass myself even more than usual. He's got me running now, five miles a day. He says it's a wonderful time for meditation. I try to meditate, but it's a little difficult, what with all the panting and the wheezing and the swollen ankles and the nausea.

Last week he took me dancing. We borrowed a car and drove to a club in Springfield. There were hundreds of us jammed in, dancing—straight couples, gay couples—and all I kept thinking was, this place has got to be a major fire hazard. We danced for four and a half hours. My hair was so wet from sweat it looked as if I'd gone swimming. When we finally left the club, I was woozy. The next day my whole body ached. But I liked the feeling.

I've been having some problems with the art class I'm taking. I mean, yes, Caravaggio's paintings are really beautiful, and the people in Poussin always seem like they're dancing, and Rubens is sumptuous; and I promise you, I really respect their talent; but the professor's always talking about how the paintings "speak to us on an emotional level." Actually, according to this guy, the paintings never shut up. I don't get it. To me, the paintings are mute—lovely, but frozen.

Louis and I decide to go to Boston to take in some museums. He's working on an essay about images of music in painting. I'm also working on a paper about music: "Some Implications of the '1/f Noise' Called Shostakovich." (I'm heavily influenced by the contributions of Voss & Clark and the Hsus, of course. Check out *Nature,* and the *Proceedings of the National Academy of Science.* You won't be disappointed.)

We get to the Gardner Museum, and Louis takes me right to a Vermeer, "The Concert." It's a strange painting, murky and quiet, but beautiful. Louis studies it for what seems like an hour, jotting down notes and muttering to himself. I find him more interesting than the painting. He's not as handsome as Simon, but his features keep changing, depending on his mood or the light. You want to keep watching, to see what's going to happen next.

Then we go to the Boston Museum of Fine Arts. We walk past painting after painting until we get to an El Greco, "Portrait of Fray Hortensio Felix de Paravicino." I stare at it, and it's almost five hundred years old, and I swear to God, it looks just like my brother Alan. He's an engineer at General Electric, in Schenectady. He's got that same black mustache and beard.

Louis tells me Paravicino was a preacher and a poet, and I believe it, this guy definitely has two sides to him. I look at the painting a little longer and suddenly I realize it looks like my father, too.

My father died when I was so young, sometimes I almost forget what he looks like. And then I'll see a photograph of him, and I'll remember right away. And I'm staring at the painting, and my eyes are starting to well up, and Louis sees that I'm almost crying, but he thinks it's because the painting is moving me. And maybe it is.

You're saying go with Louis, aren't you. Because you figure I'm too much the mathematician, and Louis is opening up a whole new side of me. But it's not that simple. Louis surprises me more, which makes him more exciting, but

Simon understands me better. At least, I think he does. I know he understands my work better.

Let's say I came home from the library and told Simon or Louis that I'd discovered a way to solve the general equation of the fifth degree—that I'd found an algebraic solution for the quintic $ax^5 + bx^4 + cx^3 + dx^2 + ex + f = 0$. (I couldn't do it, of course; Evariste Galois, building on Niels Abel's work, proved that it's impossible.) Well, Simon would jump up and down, shout, scream, he'd know that it was a great breakthrough, he'd be able to share my excitement. Louis would say, "That's great. Want to see a movie?"

I asked Louis to go with me to the math department's end-of-semester party. It'll be interesting to see how he gets along with all of us. I'm the first to admit, we mathematicians are a bunch of oddballs.

The day before my birthday, Simon was busy studying for his calculus test, and Louis was arranging a sit-in at the provost's office. He'd gotten hold of a computer printout of all the stocks owned by the university endowment and found out that Hampshire invests in some big tobacco companies.

Louis asks me if I want to come to the sit-in. I say sure. "Just make sure you bring enough cash," he tells me.

"For what?"

"For bail."

About twenty of us head to the provost's office, and then we don't leave. The provost gets madder and madder. He starts screaming and threatens to have us arrested. We still won't leave. The cops show up and try to usher us out nicely. They don't want to arrest us, but the provost insists, and since we still won't budge, the cops throw us in a paddy wagon.

We're all put in jail. The men and women are separated, and it's a little scary, and a little exciting, and very, very dirty. Finally we post bail. It's almost midnight by the time we're released. The dean, who's shown up by now, tells us we've all been put on academic probation, but none of us are expelled.

Louis asks me if I'm sorry I got involved, and I say I'm not. We kiss good night. I get to my dorm room a little after midnight, and Simon's sitting in front of my door, waiting for me.

"What are you doing here?"

"Look at your watch," he says. "Happy birthday."

He gives me three presents. One of them's circular, one of them's rectangular, one of them's triangular. We go into my room and I open the presents. The circle is a Frisbee. The rectangle is a Louis Armstrong CD. And the triangle is, well, a triangle (the kind a percussionist would use). We put on the Louis Armstrong CD, and we dance, slowly, and for a long while, but this time I don't get tired. Simon says he's going to go to the math department party, but it's right after his organic chem final, so he'll meet me there. "Great," I say, holding him, feeling him holding me.

I'm at the math department party with Louis, and we're having a good time. Louis is laughing at all of us, and I'm laughing because he's laughing, and then Simon comes up to me, and suddenly I'm not laughing anymore. Simon looks at Louis. Louis looks at Simon. And they know, immediately.

We chat for a moment or two while I struggle desperately to think of some kind of escape route, some kind of strategy. I think of telling them that they're the opposite of each other, but so exactly opposite that if I took their absolute values, in mathematical terms, they would be the same—so really there's no problem. (I think there's a problem.) Then I just run.

I run right out of the party and I run to my dorm room and I call my brother and I keep calling until finally he gets home and picks up the phone. My brother can't help me. He says they're both going to be mad at me, but if I pick one of them, he'll forgive me. He says I have to pick one or I'll lose them both. Al, I say, I can't. You have to, he says.

I hang up the phone and at first I don't know what to do. I think about Simon and how much he cares about me, how much he wants to spend time with me. And I think about Louis, how he's broken through my wall of mathematics, my armor of theorems; how he's made me see that there's more to life than set theory; how I'm not the same person at all anymore. And then I choose: Simon.

ONE CITY

It was a Saturday, and I took the B train down to Greenwich Village and then transferred to the D. I stayed on the D train a few stops and got off on Santa Monica Boulevard.

Jimmy was waiting for me on the corner of Fairfax. "Let's go see Wendy," he suggested and we headed back uptown. We drove up to Columbus Avenue and found a parking spot near Wendy's co-op. Wendy asked us where we wanted to eat, and we decided on the Carnegie Deli. The one on Seventh Avenue was too crowded, so we thought we'd try Beverly Hills. We took the M104 bus down Broadway, got off on Wilshire, and then walked from there.

Sandra Bullock and Grace Paley were eating lunch together at the deli. It was pretty exciting to see them.

I was supposed to meet some people in Hollywood after lunch. The car was still on Columbus, and anyway we figured we'd make better time if we took the subway. The IRT was packed. We ran into Ruth Brickman on the train.

"Guess who we saw at the Carnegie Deli," Wendy said.

"Grace Paley?"

"Well, yeah," Wendy admitted sourly. "How'd you know?"

"It was in the trades," Ruth said.

I met my friend Pete near Musso and Frank's. Pete had passes for all of us at the Directors Guild, on Sunset Boulevard; we got to see Arnold Schwarzenegger's remake of *Finian's Rainbow* for free. Afterward, we had a few drinks in Little Italy.

"The Dodgers and the Yankees are both in first place," Ruth said. "This could be the year."

"After all this time, a subway series," Jimmy noted.

"What a summer," I said.

We had a few more drinks.

"So, Pete," Wendy began, "I never told you. You know who—"

"Grace Paley?" guessed Pete.

"Damn," Wendy said.

It was getting late, and all of us had commutes—Pete lived in the Bronx and Jimmy lived in Burbank—but since the day had been so nice, no one wanted to cut it short.

The evening was just as glorious. Pedestrians still strolled through the streets and the restaurants remained open. People were laughing and lively, the city was brimming with activity. A breeze cooled us off while we walked. I thought I might go for a late-night swim when I got back to my apartment in the East Village. I wouldn't have time to use my pool on Sunday: in the morning I was taking a class in portfolio management at NYU, in the afternoon I had a tai chi chuan lesson in the Marina, and in the evening I was going to a concert at Lincoln Center.

"All we've done today is eat," Jimmy said.

"And star-gaze," Wendy reminded him. "Or have you forgotten Grace Paley so soon?"

Ruth said she'd go to an aerobics class early in the morning to work off the weight she'd gained.

Everyone belonged to a health club. Everyone was in great shape. Everyone had a tan. Everyone was very concerned about nutrition. Everyone walked to work wearing a business suit and sneakers. Everyone worked in the film industry. Everyone went to the Hamptons for the weekend. There was no humidity. It was never too cold. The subways ran on time.

"You know something?" Wendy said, kissing us good night. "This is really the perfect city."

THE GRANDMA GOLEM

Hanna-Botya lay in bed, moaning. Alert and nimble throughout her seventies, she had fallen in her kitchen a few weeks before her eightieth birthday and broken her hip. For four years she had remained in bed, unable to get up, slipping gradually into senility. Sometimes she recognized her daughter Rokhl; sometimes she confused Rokhl with her Aunt Leah; sometimes she mistook her daughter for Anna, the maid who helped care for her.

"Let me die," Hanna-Botya said.

Anna took a firm hand with the old woman. "Stop it, Grandma. Drink your soup, it's getting cold." Anna, a large-boned, ruddy-faced woman in her fifties, fed Hanna-Botya the soup, spoonful by spoonful—Hanna-Botya was unable to feed herself. Much of the soup dribbled down the invalid's chin.

"Salty," Hanna-Botya pronounced. Suddenly cheerful,

she grinned at the maid. Anna took a napkin and wiped Hanna-Botya's face roughly.

"Be careful," Rokhl said, coming into the room to tuck her mother in for the night. Her mother liked Anna, and rarely whimpered when she was fed or when her diapers were changed, but Rokhl wished Anna were gentler with Hanna-Botya. Still, Rokhl needed Anna's help. A small woman—smaller than her mother—Rokhl lacked the strength to turn Hanna-Botya over.

"Hello, darling," her mother greeted her.

"Do you know who I am?"

"I'm not sure," Hanna-Botya replied. "I think we're related." She began crying softly. "I don't remember."

Rokhl wiped her mother's eyes and then her own. Before becoming senile, Hanna-Botya had been a prickly, self-reliant woman, generous with her daughter and grandchildren, critical of almost everyone else. She had hated to be dependent on anyone's charity. Now her worst fear had come to pass: helpless and afraid, mewling like a newborn pup, Hanna-Botya was a burden to her family.

"I love you, Anna," Hanna-Botya told Rokhl, who pulled the blanket up over her mother and smoothed what remained of her silver hair. Hanna-Botya clutched the edge of the blanket. Her hands had grown thinner with age and her bones showed through the pale, bluish skin. "Men have it so easy." Hanna-Botya, suddenly furious, spat out the

words. "All they do is work and then they come home.
Women have it hard. What did Sam ever do for me?"

"He loved you, Mameh."

It had been a shock at first for Rokhl to hear her mother
talk so bitterly about Samuel, Rokhl's father, who was buried
in one of Kishinev's Jewish cemeteries. She had always
thought her parents had been happy together, but the last
few years she had learned how much rancor burned within
her mother. When Hanna-Botya first hurt her hip, she spent
hours in bed remembering the slights she had received from
her husband and sisters-in-law. "Dvora told me my chicken
was dry," Hanna-Botya would say, and then she'd laugh triumphantly. "Well, she's dead now, the whore."

Hanna-Botya had been a handsome woman once, but
her lips had cracked and turned blue, the skin on her nose
and cheeks had started peeling, and her hair had thinned,
exposing patches of scaly pink scalp. As her face narrowed
with age, her cheekbones became more prominent. She
looked more and more like her mother, Miriam. It was a
great surprise to Rokhl to see her grandmother's long narrow
face and pained brown eyes again after so many years.

Sora the Mute came to the house the day Hanna-Botya
caught a cold. Sora had lost her voice, and her wits, five
years earlier, after being raped by a Moldavian policeman

during the Kishinev pogrom. She lived by begging. She knocked only on Jewish homes, first running her fingers over the mezuzot outside the doors.

Sora made a moaning sound to ask for money and rubbed her belly to indicate hunger. Rokhl said she couldn't spare any change. Sora moaned louder and Rokhl, annoyed, tried to shoo her away. Sora made a fist and beat the air in anger, then became plaintive, rubbing her belly again. When Rokhl didn't respond, Sora let her fingers move down to her crotch. She spread her legs into a wider stance, moaned, and leered grotesquely at Rokhl. Rokhl slammed the door shut.

Later that day, Rokhl chastised herself for her lack of charity to poor Sora, who had been a pious woman before she was attacked. The last year had been cruel to Rokhl, and she felt herself hardening. An only child, she had no one besides Anna to help her with her mother. Her first cousin Zabalye was busy with her own mother, Hanna-Botya's sister Leah, who was bedridden as well.

Rokhl was always tired. Pensive and self-doubting, she was frustrated by her body's frailty. She had had her children late, and she felt old. Her waist was still trim, but her breasts had begun to droop, her hair had turned gray, and she had entered menopause. Her husband was no longer aroused by her—they hadn't had physical relations in months. Sometimes she thought she would go mad from the loneliness. That night, listening to her mother cough so hard it sounded like a bark, Rokhl embraced her husband, seeking only some comfort, but Avrom turned away.

The next morning the faint blue of Hanna-Botya's fingers had crept upward into her chest, throat, and face. Her thin breasts, which sagged almost to her belly, felt ice-cold to Rokhl. Anna tried to feed Hanna-Botya soup, but the old woman had trouble swallowing. In the afternoon, when Rokhl returned home from her husband's busy tailor shop, her mother looked even worse. Rokhl ran to get the doctor.

Dr. Fischer, thin, sallow, and morose, smoked too much. His fingers, stained the color of copper by tobacco, trembled as he tapped the old woman's chest and back. He diagnosed pneumonia and said there was nothing he could do. "Pneumonia is her friend," he told Rokhl, closing his brown medical bag and buckling the brass buckle. "Her last, best friend."

"Her friend?" Rokhl didn't understand.

"Your mother will die at home, with her daughter by her side. This is a good death," the doctor pronounced.

Rokhl's three children filed into the room to say good-bye to their grandmother. Dovid, named after his Great-aunt Dvora at his grandfather's insistence, kissed Hanna-Botya's blue cheek. Mikhail kissed her blue hand. But Margolit, the youngest and only girl, was too frightened of her grand-mother's rasping breath to approach the dying woman.

Hanna-Botya reached out to touch Margolit, but the girl backed away.

Then, with a tremendous struggle, Hanna-Botya sat up in bed. She seemed for a moment to regain her old alertness and intelligence. With anguished eyes, Hanna-Botya looked at her daughter Rokhl.

"What is it, Mameh? What do you want?"

"Want . . ." Her voice was no more than a whisper.

"What?"

"I want . . ." Hanna-Botya took a painful gulp of air.

"What?"

"To read . . ." Hanna-Botya moaned and sank back down into the bed.

Rokhl could hardly swallow. "Oh, Mameh."

"Don't cry," Hanna-Botya tried to console her. "Leah, don't cry . . ." And then words failed her, and she began coughing again.

Her mother had never learned to read—Hanna-Botya's father had forbidden her to go to cheder. Rokhl had never learned either. It was the great shame of her life that she couldn't help Dovid, Mikhail, and now Margolit with their homework. The boys had tried to teach her to read, but she always felt stupid and tired, and the words didn't come easily. Margolit had just started learning the aleph-bet. Perhaps Margolit would prove a better teacher.

———

Rokhl and Anna sat up with Hanna-Botya, whose breathing grew increasingly arduous. Around three in the morning, against her will, Rokhl fell asleep. Anna stayed up and prayed.

She prayed for Hanna-Botya's recovery, even though she knew the old woman wanted to die. Anna needed the job: work was scarce, and it would be difficult to find another position. She wasn't young anymore. She didn't know how old she was exactly, but she thought she had been eight or nine when the serfs were emancipated.

Hardworking and devout, homely and deliberate, Anna was raising her granddaughter, Marya, by herself. Her daughter had run off to the Ukraine with a retired first mate who said he was a speculator in the sugar markets but was actually, Anna was sure, a gambler and a drunk. Marya had no one but Anna to provide for her.

"Don't die, Grandma," Anna hissed at the old woman. "Don't you dare die."

Hanna-Botya's head was thrown back. Her breath was almost imperceptible. Anna knew Hanna-Botya's soul was preparing to leave her body. "You're not going anywhere," she whispered angrily. She drew a secret symbol on a slip of paper and placed the paper on the invalid's tongue, like a communion wafer. She dropped water on Hanna-Botya's forehead, then lit a match and held it close to the water until the water almost sizzled. Her great-grandmother had taught her this charm to ward off the death-spirits.

Anna blew out the match, wiped off the water, then grabbed hold of Hanna-Botya's arm and prayed again. She breathed her great-grandmother's secret name for God into the nostrils of her patient. Hanna-Botya moaned and shivered. Her soul fought to escape from her body—but Anna fought too. Hanna-Botya's soul shrieked silently, begging to be released—but Anna wouldn't relent. She only grasped the old woman's arm tighter. Finally, in its desperate attempt to flee, Hanna-Botya's soul was rent from her life-spirit; the soul escaped from the body, but the life-spirit, trapped by Anna, remained behind, separated for the first time from its twin.

Rokhl twitched in her sleep. She dreamed that she was at her mother's elaborate funeral and that the coffin was open. She walked up to the casket and looked in. She saw her mother lying in the pine box, peaceful and content, but with a large crucifix around her neck. Rokhl woke with a start and looked at her mother.

Hanna-Botya was breathing more easily. Her eyes were open but strangely vacant.

"I saved her," Anna said gleefully. She had already removed the paper from the old woman's tongue. "I did it."

And Rokhl felt a confusing sense of happiness, helplessness, and rage. Her mother had passed out of danger.

Hanna-Botya continued to gain strength the next few days. She was ravenously hungry. Anna fed her bowl after bowl of soup, then fed her gruel, then cut her small pieces of meat. Hanna-Botya's thin fingers grew thick and powerful.

She had changed since recovering from the pneumonia. She was practically mute now. She understood what Anna or Rokhl said but almost never responded. Her eyes followed them around the room, but they were the eyes of a wolf, wary and shrewd. She still had most of her teeth, and these looked sharper and longer. And Hanna-Botya was angry; Rokhl and Anna feared that she would snap at them or perhaps even become violent.

Her whole body had taken on a bluish hue, although she was breathing quite easily. She looked larger—not just heavier, but taller and more powerful. Even Anna had a difficult time turning her over to change her diapers.

Queerest of all was the bruise that had appeared on Hanna-Botya's forehead. At first the blemish looked like a black-and-blue mark, and Rokhl wondered how her mother had hurt herself. Over time the splotch seemed to shift, spreading out into a dim pattern. Rokhl thought the bruise might now resemble Hebrew letters, but she couldn't be sure, and she thought her husband or sons would laugh at her if she mentioned her concern.

Rokhl was making tsimmes in the kitchen when she heard a shuffling sound behind her. She turned around and gasped. It was her mother, wearing only a thin nightgown, walking slowly toward her—her mother, who hadn't left her bed in four years.

"She wanted to get up," explained Anna, bewildered, following behind.

Her mother looked large—larger than Rokhl remembered, but of course she hadn't seen her standing in a long time.

"Hun-gry," Hanna-Botya said, having a hard time with the word.

"I'm just making some tsimmes . . ."

"Hun-gry!" Hanna-Botya shouted.

Rokhl ran to the cupboard and took out some challah and some salted fish. Hanna-Botya ate the food in a few huge gulps.

"More!"

Rokhl had been saving a pie for later, but she cut a large piece for her mother and served it to her with a fork. Her mother threw the silverware on the floor, ate the slice with her bare hands, and then attacked the rest of the pie.

"More!" Hanna-Botya cried again. "Now!"

"Mameh," Rokhl said softly and reasonably, although she was shaking inside, "you'll have to wait until I finish the tsimmes."

Hanna-Botya, annoyed, mumbled to herself, but she sat at the table and waited for Rokhl to serve her.

Mendel Hirschbein knocked at the back door while Rokhl was cooking. Mendel came from an intelligent family—his brother was a rabbi—but he had fallen down a flight of stairs when he was nine years old and his mind had never matured properly. He still had a large scar over his left eyebrow from the accident. Cheerful and hugely fat, he visited Jewish homes looking for food and performed odd jobs to make money. Now in his forties, he had a full black beard flecked with gray whiskers, a forehead furrowed with worry lines, and a child's eager, innocent eyes.

"Can I eat here?" Mendel asked. "Please?"

Rokhl had always liked Mendel, but she hadn't gone to the market that day and she worried that she wouldn't have enough food for the rest of her family. "Mendel, I'm sorry. Today's not a good day."

Hanna Botya was furious. "He eat!" she screamed. "He eat!"

"All right, Mameh, all right. Sit down, Mendel." Rokhl went into her bedroom, closed the door behind her, and took out some of the money she had hidden at the bottom of her cedar chest. She closed the cedar chest silently, smoothed its blue slipcover, and left the room. She gave the money to Anna and told her to go to the store.

Rokhl returned to the kitchen and prepared two large plates of tsimmes for her mother and Mendel. They devoured the food.

"That was good!" Mendel said after he had finished, smacking his lips.

"Good!" Hanna-Botya agreed, laughing.

Rokhl sat at the table, next to her mother. She looked at the wound over her mother's eyes. "Mameh, what does that say?" For now Rokhl was sure the splotch was forming letters. She touched the bruise gently.

"No!" Her mother screamed and pushed her away. "No touch!"

Rokhl was too shocked to cry. "You hit me, Mameh."

"Let me see," Mendel said. He moved closer to Hanna-Botya. "Aleph." He touched the letter. Hanna-Botya recoiled, then allowed him to touch her. "Mem." He touched the next letter. "Suf." He touched the final letter. "Emes. I know that word," Mendel said proudly.

"Emes?" Rokhl repeated, stunned. The word meant "truth" in Hebrew and Yiddish.

Her mother got up from the table and walked back to her bedroom, her nightgown billowing from the draft through the kitchen.

"Mendel," said Rokhl, shivering, but not from the draft, "go get the rabbi."

Mendel returned with his older brother, Rabbi Hirschbein. The rabbi, who had some of Mendel's girth and the same furrowed forehead, stroked his gray beard and chewed his bottom lip while inspecting the old woman, now asleep in her bed.

"Emes," he agreed.

"What does it mean?" Rokhl asked anxiously. "Is it the devil?"

"Not at all. The Talmud says, the seal of God is truth. God is here, not the devil," the rabbi comforted her. "Now tell me what happened."

Rokhl described her mother's bout with pneumonia, her near death, and then her miraculous recovery.

"Strange," mused Rabbi Hirschbein. "I think she was ready to die. Something pulled her back. Perhaps some task she hadn't completed, a debt she hadn't repaid . . . I think that must be it. There was a case like this in Sevastopol. My cousin, Rabbi Schneiderman, told me."

"What happened?"

"An old man's soul left his body. But he was still alive."

Rokhl was perplexed. "What is a body without a soul?"

"Well, not a Jew, that much is certain."

"My mother isn't Jewish?"

"Not any longer."

"Well then, what is she?" asked Rokhl, afraid.

The rabbi paused before answering her. "She's one of God's creatures," he said at last. "You must love her and feed her and honor her."

But Rokhl knew the word Rabbi Hirschbein wouldn't utter. Her mother was a golem: an unformed substance, a stupid person, an artificial woman—a monster.

"I don't have to honor her," Rokhl said tearfully. "She's not my mother anymore."

"It doesn't matter who she is. Charity equals all the other commandments," the rabbi said.

Rokhl's husband, Avrom, sipped his hot soup slowly, watching his mother-in-law eat. Listless and somber, he had a grim, stolid face, with thick heavy eyelids. He resented supporting Hanna-Botya, but he had long ago decided that when his good and bad deeds were tallied in the Book of Judgment, the money he had spent on his mother-in-law would count as tzedakah, or charity to the poor, which he was obligated to give.

Hanna-Botya had risen from bed to join them for dinner. There seemed to be no end to her appetite. Finishing her soup, she turned and caught sight of him looking at her. She looked back at him with her dull, empty eyes. Finally he felt frightened and looked away. She cackled triumphantly, like a child winning a game of draidl.

After she ate, she walked back to her bedroom, taking small, shuffling steps.

"Good night, Mameh," Rokhl called after her.

Her mother turned around and looked at her curiously. "Night," Hanna-Botya said flatly. It had an oddly sarcastic ring.

"The neighbors are already talking," Avrom said later. "It's bad for business."

"It's not my fault," Rokhl said quickly, but the truth was, she felt guilty. She blamed herself for falling asleep the night her mother almost passed away. Perhaps if she'd stayed up, she could have held her mother's hand, soothed her, eased her into the next world.

"Do you know how much money we're spending on food?" Avrom complained.

The next day, Rokhl's mother began leaving the house, foraging the neighborhood for food. Hanna-Botya accompanied Mendel and Sora the Mute on their begging rounds. She even ate pork. Rokhl thought the shame of it would kill her.

"Don't eat pork, Mameh," Rokhl begged her. "It's not kosher."

But her mother only laughed at her.

Hanna-Botya was getting younger. Her hair was fuller and had turned from silver to shiny black. The wrinkles on her face were smoothing, so that the letters spelling *emes* stood out in bold Prussian-blue relief on her forehead. Hunched over for years, she could now hold herself erect.

And Hanna-Botya was growing. She towered over Rokhl, over Avrom even. She stood over six feet tall, strong, healthy, brooding, powerful—and hungry, always.

The whole Jewish quarter of Kishinev bruited rumors about Rokhl's mother. The neighbors said Hanna-Botya was possessed by a dybbuk. They said she was having unlawful relations with Mendel Hirschbein and whispered among themselves about even more perverse relations with Sora the Mute.

Hanna-Botya came home rarely, and only to eat. Painful as it was to see her, Rokhl fed her out of a sense of duty, remembering the rabbi's instructions. This monster, this sham mother, had once been her real mother—a difficult mother, sometimes, but tender, too. Rokhl kept a clean bed ready for Hanna-Botya, but her mother preferred to sleep in an abandoned barn a mile away.

Hanna-Botya lived in the barn with the drunks and the

whores and the anarchist, Chaim-Yitzkhok Perlmutter. The building was filthy. The walls were smeared with dirt and dung, the passageways covered with cobwebs. The soft rain soaked the wood boards and left them moldy. Chicken feathers, gathered and clumped into pillows, littered the floor. Wind whistled through the boarded windows, but little light filtered through.

Chaim-Yitzkhok had worked for ten years in a sugar plant in the Ukraine before returning home to Kishinev to spread the gospel of insurrection. He was a skinny, bowlegged redhead with a red beard, a red, peeling nose, and fair, freckled skin. Clubbed on the legs by police during the 1905 revolution, Chaim-Yitzkhok walked with a limp. Hanna-Botya followed him around the city when she wasn't looking for food. When he addressed small crowds, she bobbed her head and torso rhythmically, pleased, as though she were davening in synagogue. Sometimes, as his speech reached its passionate crescendo, she hugged herself tight and gasped with pleasure. At night he was teaching the prostitutes and her to read.

Hanna-Botya was eating pot roast at home when a neighbor came by to tell Rokhl that her Aunt Leah had died. Rokhl hurried over to her cousin Zabalye's house to help. Hanna-Botya came with her, although Rokhl wanted her mother to stay behind. The two cousins embraced. The burial society had already sewn a shroud for Leah out of white linen and laid the body on a long board for the ritual cleansing. Hanna-Botya stood in front of Leah's mirror, staring at her reflection and at the letters on her forehead until the mirror was covered with mourning paper. Rokhl stopped the clocks and lit candles at the head of her aunt. Hanna-Botya sat down at her sister's side, patted Zabalye's dog on the head, and remained there, silent, until the body was removed.

The sexton recited, "Charity saves from death, charity saves from death," while the corpse was carried to the cemetery. The men walked behind the sexton, and the women walked behind the men. Hanna-Botya, huge and unkempt, was last in the procession. Agitated, she mumbled loudly to herself and squeezed her breasts. Her daughter was mortified, but she stopped, waited for the other women to pass, and then walked beside her mother, hoping to quiet her. Hanna-Botya allowed Rokhl to take her arm.

The mourners asked forgiveness of the deceased and the corpse was lowered into the grave. A small piece of wood was placed in each of Leah's hands; a shard of earthenware was placed on each eye. Planks of wood covered the body, then dirt covered the planks. The men took turns shoveling soil into the grave. Rokhl wanted to take a turn, too, for in some congregations women were allowed to participate, but Avrom stopped her. When Hanna-Botya reached for the shovel, the rabbi pushed her back. Insulted, Hanna-Botya moaned loudly. The rabbi recited over her protests, "From dust you came and to dust you return. Blessed be the true judge." Hanna-Botya screamed at the rabbi, "Liar! Liar!" Rokhl and the other congregants tried to ignore her. While the mourners recited the Kaddish, Hanna-Botya lay down, banging her fists against the ground and sobbing. She reminded Rokhl of her daughter, Margolit, who had thrown temper tantrums as a small child. Rokhl went to comfort her mother, but Hanna-Botya lashed out at her, biting her arm. Rokhl wept. Her mother got to her feet, bared her sharp teeth, and growled at them all. The head of the burial society tore Zabalye's dress as a sign of mourning. Hanna-Botya looked down at her own clothing—she was wearing Chaim-Yitzkhok's pants and shirt, because they were the only things that fit—and suddenly ripped open her shirt, revealing her large, full breasts.

The rabbi went over to Hanna-Botya to cover her. She began beating his chest brutally. "Liar! Liar!" she screamed again. She grabbed a handful of dirt from her sister's grave and flung it at the mourners. Rokhl, still crying, was struck in the face by the soil. Then Hanna-Botya ran away.

Rokhl, hysterical, was carried to her bed. She felt immobile; her legs wouldn't obey her. She slipped in and out of cruel, punishing dreams; she failed to recognize her chil-

dren, confusing Margolit with Mikhail, and Dovid with her
husband; at times she hallucinated. Dr. Fischer diagnosed a
brain fever, brought on by Leah's death and Hanna-Botya's
gruesome transformation. Anna was fetched to take care of
the patient.

A few days later, Hanna-Botya returned to the house to
snack. Now nearly seven feet tall, Hanna-Botya was still
wearing Chaim-Yitzkhok's pants, which extended only to her
knees, like a cheder boy's breeches. A whore at the barn had
cut her hair short, at Hanna-Botya's request. Except for her
high, full bosom, Hanna-Botya looked like a man.

Anna served her a bowl of oatmeal, but Hanna-Botya
flung the plate against the wall, shattering it. "Meat!" she
shouted.

In the next room, the children had been sitting on the
floor, playing with wooden tiles. The tiles had Hebrew letters
painted on them. The children dropped their game and ran
to the kitchen to see what had caused the commotion.
Startled by Hanna-Botya's appearance, Dovid and Mikhail
greeted their grandmother warily. Margolit, cowering, hid
behind her brothers and didn't speak at all.

"Go back to your game," Anna said.

"Stupid girl," Hanna-Botya said.

The children left the room. "I'll give you some meat,"
Anna told Hanna-Botya. She had just made chicken soup for
Rokhl, who couldn't keep any solid food down and now was

refusing to eat at all. Anna removed the drumsticks and breasts from the copper pot with a pair of tongs and served the meat to Hanna-Botya. "Here, you old witch."

"Pork?" Hanna-Botya asked hopefully.

"No, Grandma, not in this house." While Hanna-Botya gorged herself, Anna ladled out a bowl of soup and brought it to Rokhl.

"I don't want any," Rokhl said.

Hanna-Botya walked into the room. Surprised to see her daughter in bed, she grumbled to herself and sat beside Rokhl.

"Why don't you show your mother how you can eat?" Anna prompted Rokhl.

"No."

"Be a good girl," Anna said.

"I don't want any. Mameh," Rokhl said, moaning, "I don't want any."

Anna held Rokhl's nose. Tears formed in the corners of Rokhl's eyes and then ran down her cheeks. Finally, gasping, Rokhl opened her mouth. Anna quickly shoveled in some soup, forced her mouth shut, pushed her chin up, and watched her swallow. "That's a good girl. We used to do this to geese, to fatten them up."

"Mameh, help me," Rokhl cried.

Hanna-Botya said nothing, but watched her daughter intently.

"Here's another spoonful," Anna said.

"I don't want it."

"But if you don't eat, you're going to die," Anna reasoned with her. "Please? Won't you eat something?"

"No . . ."

Anna pinced Rokhl's nostrils together, and waited for Rokhl to open her mouth. But Hanna-Botya surprised Anna. The giantess grasped Anna's arm tightly and forced her to let go of Rokhl.

"You're hurting me!" Anna cried.

Hanna-Botya put her hands around Anna's throat. "Stupid maid! Stupid maid!" she shouted. Rokhl, who tried to protest, fell back in a faint.

Anna couldn't breathe or speak. She heard herself make gurgling noises. With her eyes she pled for Hanna-Botya to let go, but Hanna-Botya wouldn't release her. With her arms she beat against Hanna-Botya, but the giantess was too strong. Finally Anna suffocated.

"Stupid maid," Hanna-Botya repeated. She pushed the body under Rokhl's bed, but one of Anna's feet got stuck on the corner of the cedar chest. Hanna-Botya seemed to see the chest for the first time. She took the blue cover off and opened it. Inside she found Rokhl's cache of money. Hanna-Botya stuffed some coins in her pocket for Chaim-Yitzkhok and the prostitutes.

"I'm home, Anna," Avrom called from the kitchen. Hanna-Botya left Rokhl and the corpse and walked back into the kitchen. Avrom, facing away from his mother-in-law, was tasting the chicken soup. "It needs more salt," Avrom said petulantly. "Can't you do anything right?"

Hanna-Botya picked up the cleaver Anna had used to cut the chicken. She walked up to Avrom and sank the cleaver in the back of his skull. Avrom collapsed without making a sound.

"Stupid man," Hanna-Botya pronounced. She cut off one of his hands and threw it into the pot of chicken soup. "Meat," she said, satisfied. She put down the cleaver and rested her head on her hands at the kitchen table. She drowsed dreamlessly for a few minutes.

In the other room, Margolit, still playing, burst into laughter. Hanna-Botya was startled by the noise. She got up from her chair, picked up the pair of brass tongs on the counter, and marched slowly toward Margolit. She stood over the children, who were lost in their word game.

"I need an aleph!" Margolit said. "Why can't I ever get an aleph?" Just then, she sensed she was being watched and looked up at her grandmother. Margolit screamed.

Hanna-Botya smiled. She took the tongs, placed them on the aleph on her forehead, and pulled with all her might. The letter came loose, along with skin and skull and brains.

The two letters remaining on her forehead, the mem and the suf, now spelled met, the Hebrew word for "dead." The grandma golem crumbled into a soft pile of moist ash at the feet of her granddaughter. A few gold coins gleamed underneath the ash.

HARD BARGAINS

1.

José Pereira, Laura's editor, was a swarthy, owlish-looking man in his fifties who smelled of menthol cough drops and navel oranges. He peeled the oranges carefully, scraping away excess pith with a small knife which he kept in his desk and rinsed each morning in the men's room. He was an uninspired but self-assured editor who brooked no opposition from the reporters. They called him Uncle Joe—as in Stalin.

Although Latino, surely, Pereira seemed oddly cut off from any ethnic ties. There was a small apartment some-where, a divorce, a daughter in Aurora; black coffee, ciga-rettes, those cough drops and oranges, Monday hangovers. He liked working nights. He spoke quietly, with no real accent except the sharp, pinched Chicago inflection Laura Lerner heard all around her. She was afraid of him—afraid he would say something hurtful and accurate about her. He had already told her that she used too many semicolons. He described her, to her face, as a sheltered Catholic schoolgirl from the suburbs who would never make it in Chicago. "I'm from New York City," she said. "And I'm Jewish."

"Congratulations," was his stubborn, nasal reply.

The City News Bureau, a peculiar Chicago institution, was owned jointly by the *Sun-Times* and the *Tribune* and distributed articles to those papers as well as wire services and broadcast stations. Laura had started there ten months ago, right out of Northwestern. She had proceeded from high school to college with some confidence but found a host of childhood anxieties returning as soon as she began to work: what she should wear, whether she had said something stupid, if people liked her.

"Lerner, sweetheart, get over here."

Laura stood in front of Pereira's desk, annoyed and tired. She was stuck working nights again. "What?"

"Two kids got shot at Stateway Gardens. Black, probably. Dead, most likely. Find out for sure." José gave her a slip of yellow paper and told her to get a reaction from the family.

Laura looked at the paper. The boys had the same last name, Jarrett, and address. "A reaction?"

José didn't answer. He had already turned his attention to the article in front of him, which he read with great disdain. In the telephone directory, Laura found a number for a G. Jarrett, who lived at Stateway Gardens. She dialed, hoping a friend or neighbor would answer the phone. Instead she reached George Jarrett, the boys' father.

"They shot em. They both gone," Jarrett said calmly. "Troy, he was the older, he favored his mama's side. And Taj, my younger boy, he looked like, well, he looked like Troy. Good boys, both of em. Troy, now, he was a year older, he play trombone and he sing. His mama say he gon be another Billy Eckstine, cause she love Billy. But Troy, he wasn't no good. And Taj, well, we ain't never know what Taj was gon do, cause, well, we just ain't never know."

"Do you have any other children?"

"No."

"Mr. Jarrett, are you black?" She knew the answer but had to ask anyway since no one from the police precinct had called her back with the offical report.

"Yes, I am."

"How long have you lived there?"

"Goin on fo' years. I work part-time. I work security over at the car wash. Been working real regular past two years. We was gon move—oh God," he cried suddenly and then continued, scarcely pausing. "We was thinking real serious about moving. For the boys, you know. Cause this ain't no place to raise children. Now, well, I guess it don't matter cause—oh dear Lord, my boys, my boys," he sobbed. "You see, it just don't matter," he finished.

She felt sick to her stomach, but she had a few more questions. "Mr. Jarrett, when is the funeral?"

"Oh, on Friday. Would you like to come?"

"Oh, I wouldn't want to be a bother—"

"Cause you been listening real good and I would like you to see all the friends my, my boys had."

"Mr. Jarrett, do you know who shot your sons?" she asked.

"Crackheads. Shot em like they was hunting birds. Down there in front of the building. My boys, they was just standing there, minding they bidness."

After he told her where the services would be held, she called the police precinct again, and then she looked up Billy Eckstine in one of the reference books in the bureau's library. She had heard his name before and, assuming the name was spelled Eckstein, was surprised Mr. Jarrett had singled out a Jewish musician. When she realized her mistake she ended up reading the entire entry on Eckstine, until Pereira barked quietly at her and she got back to work.

In the early morning, before sunrise, she took the broad elevator down to the beige lobby with its chipped marble pillars and stained, worn Carrara-marble floor (the building was supposed to be renovated soon), passed beneath the huge clock glowing outside, and walked down Wacker Drive toward Michigan Avenue. Chicago was a city of clocks, a city, like New York, of deadlines and aggressive energy—but perhaps even more formidable than New York, because in Chicago you had to be aggressive and polite at the same time. Laura was the same way, driven and soft-spoken, assertive yet shy. Whenever she played tennis or pool, she became fiercely competitive; she took books out of the library to improve her game; but she apologized for winning.

It was already April but an icy wind was blowing—''Oh man, the hawk kickin' me today,'' the superintendent of her apartment building would say. The Chicago River, to her left, was still dyed green from St. Patrick's Day, although it was too dark for her to see. On the opposite bank of the river, trucks pulled up to the *Sun-Times* building, their engines groaning, at this distance, like old men getting out of bed.

It had rained during the night and the pavement was wet. She stepped over a puddle that was debating whether to freeze and entered the saunalike warmth of a Greek coffee shop that was always open. Another thing about Chicago: no one ever turned the thermostat down. Laura sat under a new campaign poster for George Dukakis and ordered oatmeal and coffee, orange juice, and toast slathered with butter and jam. She hoped to stuff down her frustration along with the meal.

When she had told José that she had been invited to the funeral, he had informed her, as she knew he would, that she would be attending. She didn't want to go. She wondered now if she had told him out of a sense of dutifulness, or if she wanted to punish herself for intruding on the Jarretts' lives, or if she had simply been hungry for a good feature story.

2.

Laura was the only white in the congregation. George Jarrett introduced himself immediately. When he invited her to come back to his apartment for refreshments, she heard an invisible José Pereira hissing in her ear: "Would you go already!"

Mr. Jarrett's brother-in-law, Mr. Williams, an optician with grown children, gave her a lift in his town car to Stateway Gardens, a crumbling housing project at 39th and Princeton. They drove down broken streets, the huge car disdaining the potholes. She began to interview him—her usual response to awkward social situations.

His children, a boy and a girl, were both doctors. "My wife passed last year," Mr. Williams said. "Right about this time last year. You see, she wanted to hold on until Easter. She was very strong."

"I'm sorry."

"You see, she was sick for a long time. . . . So we were prepared. Not like this." He told her that June, his late wife's sister, had lost her father, her sister, and now her children in the last two years. At the funeral, Mrs. Jarrett, ruined and desperate, her wide eyes swelled nearly shut from crying, collapsed during the minister's eulogy, falling on the floor of the church.

"I had to hide the newspaper from George and June," Mr. Williams said. "But you know they're going to hear about it. It said those boys might be mixed up in drugs. I don't believe it, they were good boys. Was that your paper?"

"Yes," Laura said softly.

"Why'd they have to write something like that? Those boys are dead, they can't hurt anybody."

Laura, looking out the window, didn't respond.

"Who wrote that article anyway? I should give him a piece of my mind. I should write him a letter."

They passed two boys skateboarding past a dripping fire hydrant and dilapidated storefronts. "I wrote it," Laura said. They drove in silence the rest of the way.

The Jarretts lived in one of the high-rises at Stateway Gardens. Small children were jumping in puddles in front of the building, where Troy and Taj had been shot. The children stopped speaking when Laura passed by. Mr. Williams led her inside, through the harsh yellow light of the dirty brown lobby, past the broken mailboxes, an overflowing garbage can, and a man nodding off in a plastic chair. They waited a long time at a bank of elevators. Only one of the elevators was working.

The door to the Jarretts' apartment was closed but she could hear crying within. Someone opened the door for them and then she entered the apartment. The rooms were small, square, drafty. None of the closets had doors. White sheets hung over the closets and gray sheets partly covered the battered sofa and chairs. In the tiny kitchen, food had been set out on the table: chicken, ham, string beans, biscuits, rice, salad, orange Kool-Aid, pies. Mrs. Jarrett sat at the table, weeping into a napkin, staring at her paper plate. Her friends and relatives tried to comfort her. In the living room, where the younger people had gathered, the clay California raisins gamboled merrily on the large television set. Mr. Jarrett sat with the boys and girls, explaining how the raisins were animated, periodically wiping his eyes.

The older women were gathered in Mr. and Mrs. Jarrett's small bedroom, sitting on mismatched bridge chairs. Mrs. Jarrett's mother, Mrs. Easley, talked to some of her friends there. She encouraged Laura to sit with them. "My husband worked six days a week and nights too," she told Laura. "It was a different world. People paid their bills. We didn't need no handouts."

"Mmm-hmm," another woman said.

"So things have changed?" Laura prompted, taking her notebook out of her bag.

"Oh yes. It's a new and ugly world. God is testing us, that's what I believe. Jesus is a teacher and Jesus taught us right from wrong. But He's a hard grader, too." Mrs. Easley watched, approvingly, as Laura took notes. "All around me," she said, "I see people failing."

"Why is that, do you think?"

"The drugs," she snapped. "And the pornography."

"That's right," a woman said.

"And low expectations. I taught Sunday school and I expected my students to learn. I didn't hope, I expected. And people nowadays have no expectations for their children."

Later Laura went into the boys' bedroom, a small, ordinary room with basketball posters Scotch-taped to the wall, a single chest of drawers, two beds with gray army surplus blankets, a small television set. A boy, perhaps fifteen years old, sat alone on the bare floor, watching the television set with the sound turned off, his shoulders twitching. He turned to look at her. "What you want?"

"Why is the sound off?"

"It broke."

The boy, Dion, was the first cousin of Troy and Taj, the son of another of June Jarrett's sisters. He lived with his mother in the same building. His shoulders continued to twitch and his eyes were bloodshot, although he wasn't crying. He resembled Mrs. Jarrett, with the same wide face and eyes.

Laura wondered when she could leave. Finally, after an

hour, she asked if she could call a cab. Mrs. Easley said that
the cabs never came and besides it was too expensive and
anyway her grandson would make sure she got home safely.
Laura had hoped, selfishly, that someone might drive her.
"Dion," Mrs. Easley called.

"I got to be here," he objected at once. "You know I
do."

"You make sure Miz Lerner gets home," she said.

"She say she want to call a cab . . ."

"You take her right now," Mrs. Easley said.

"But she say . . ."

"Thank you."

As they walked to the el stop two blocks away, Dion
looked behind them nervously, as if afraid they were being
followed. He wouldn't let her pay for him. On board the
el, he made sure there was an empty seat between them. He
stared absently at the advertising placards, but turned toward
the door at the first stop as passengers boarded. She would
have felt safer without him.

"Did your cousins look like you?" Laura finally asked
him, her curiosity overcoming her caution. He ignored her.

Four teenage boys, sprawled over the seats opposite her,
heckled one another loudly and stared at Laura. She had a
bad headache. She wished she'd taken a cab. At the next
stop, a husky black man, carrying a large white Styrofoam

cup in which some change jiggled, stepped into the train. He wore a dark knit cap and a grimy down vest tearing at the armpits. Greeting them all loudly, he offered to tell them jokes in exchange for money. "What kind of animal can tell time?" he began. He directed the joke at Laura.

No one answered.

"What kind of an animal can tell time? I'll tell you. It's a watchdog."

The boys groaned.

"Why should you stare at your container of orange juice for at least half an hour every morning?" he asked Laura.

"Cause you be livin' on a train and it the only food you got," one of the boys proposed.

"Why should you stare at your orange juice? Because it says 'concentrate.' "

The boys liked this joke but wouldn't give him any money. The husky man approached Laura, who found a quarter in her coat pocket and dropped it into his cup. He looked inside the cup. "A quarter? That's all you got? Those were good jokes." Laura didn't want to open her wallet on the train, but she found some more change in her pockets and gave it to him. "God bless you," the man said.

Their train slowed to a stop and then idled for twenty minutes. They waited and the boys cursed. The lights went out and the boys hooted and one of them said, "We comin' for you now.'' She sensed Dion stiffening near her, which meant he was nervous too, which made her more afraid. The lights came back on and the train wheezed backward into a station. The speakers mumbled something about a breakdown up ahead. All of the passengers were ordered out. Dion walked behind Laura, at a distance.

The passengers scattered, most walking to the exits, a few waiting for the next train. When the other boys were gone, Laura spoke to Dion. ''I want to take a cab.''

''I ain't stopping you.''

The sun had set. They emerged from the station into a dingy street in a terrible neighborhood of vacant lots, boarded-up houses, and gutted buildings. It had started to rain again. At the corner she saw a neon beer sign pulsing in the darkness. ''I'll call a cab from there.''

''Mmm-hmm.'' He followed behind her until she reached the bar. ''I done what she say,'' he told her. ''Don't you be saying I didn't. If she ask, you tell her.''

''I really appreciate—''

He was already walking away.

3.

She opened the door. A radio somewhere was tuned to a jazz station, and for a moment no one spoke, so that the half-dozen men inside might almost have been listening to the music in silence, as if they were attending a concert. An older man with ebony skin, gray hair, and a gray mustache looked up at her and squinted. He was sitting at a card table near the door, doing paperwork under the light of a small yellow desk lamp. "You must be in the wrong place." He laughed. "Child, you done got lost."

Her eyes were getting used to the darkness. "Excuse me, is there a pay phone here?"

"Yes there is."

"Oh good—"

"But it don't work." More laughter. "Who you want to call?"

"Her boyfriend," someone called out from the bar, stepping toward her, into the light. The skin on his throat, chin, and part of his cheek was covered by a mottled blemish of gray pigment, as if someone had splashed him with paint.

She turned back to the older man. "A cab," she said.

"Mmm-hmm. That's a good idea. I'll do it for you cause you so sweet." He rose slowly and limped past the pool tables into a private office at the back. He closed the door behind him.

The bartender looked at her sourly. A tall, bearded, middle-aged man, he wore a clean white apron, starched stiff as cardboard. Laura's eyes traveled up to the mirror behind and above him. She saw what he was seeing, a frightened schoolgirl lost on a class trip. She smoothed her wet hair nervously. Her head was throbbing. "You a college girl?" the bartender asked.

She didn't know if he was asking if she had attended college in the past or if she was still going, but she nodded anyway.

"What's the capital of Burkina Faso?"

"I don't know."

"Ouagadougou. Don't they teach you that?"

She didn't answer.

"You know where Burkina Faso is?" he asked her.

"Africa?"

"Africa," he said.

Uncertain what to do, she wandered, as in a daze, over to a pool table in the center of the room and touched the rail with her hand. A wiry man with coppery skin, coppery hair, and yellowish eyes was chalking his cue stick on the other side of the table. "You play eight ball?" he asked her.

"I played—a little—yes," she stammered. He put a five-dollar bill on the rail. "Oh, I don't want to bet," she said. He waited patiently. They all waited. She opened her bag and then her wallet and took out five singles, which she placed carefully on top of his bill.

"You can break," he said. She took off her coat, placing it on top of a worn wooden chair and hiding her bag underneath it. He passed her another cue. She found a pad of Scotch Brite and rubbed the shaft a few times. *Here I was,* Laura narrated to herself, rehearsing the surreal story she would tell her friends, *alone on the South Side, playing pool.* The door to the back office opened and the older man returned. ''I called,'' he said.

She thought she'd be rusty but she got a decent break, sinking the three ball in a side pocket, then shooting the six ball low, with draw, so that the cue ball bounced back after sinking the six and she had a better shot at the four ball. She shot and sank the four with low right English, the English pulling the cue ball back so that she had a chance at making the five ball. She shot again but missed the five.

The light-skinned man was a good player. Although she hadn't given him very good position he managed to sink the eleven, the thirteen, the fourteen, and the fifteen before missing the nine. The men in the pool hall murmured their approval each time he pocketed a ball.

The crowd, she narrated, *was against me.*

''What's your name?'' she asked her opponent.

''Henry.''

''I'm Laura.''

''Uh huh.''

She sank the five and the two but had no chance at the one or the seven. Henry pocketed another ball before missing a difficult off-the-rail bank shot. She sank the one, the seven, and then the eight ball. Only after she stood up from her crouch did she become aware of the silence, the unnerving silence, cold and dangerous, that had gradually thickened the air. She asked herself how she could have been so stupid as to win. "Sorry. I, I got lucky," she said.

The older man, shaking his head, picked up a broom and started sweeping the floor.

"Again," Henry said, putting a ten-dollar bill on the rail, on top of the five and the ones. "You got time."

She sank a ball on the break and quickly pocketed two more. Then she missed deliberately.

"You letting me win, Miss Ann?"

"No, I'm off, I have a headache—"

"So if I win it's cause you ain't feeling good."

"That's, that's not . . ."

"You think I need your help? Girl, I don't need nothing from you."

"He don't need nothing," chorused the man with the blemish.

The older man coughed and kept sweeping, knocking the broom hard against one of the tables.

Henry won easily. "We got to play again," he said. "We even."

Laura looked at the older man. "Why is it taking so long?"

"Child, you ain't on Lake Shore Drive," he said, but not unkindly.

"There it is, heh heh," someone else at the bar chortled. He was a short, burly man with huge biceps stretching the sleeves of his white T-shirt. "They on C.P. Time round here."

Henry knocked on the pile of bills and she had to hunt through her wallet for a twenty. She couldn't find one.

"How you paying for the cab," the bartender demanded.

"I don't know," she said with mounting anxiety.

She remembered an emergency twenty hidden at the bottom of her bag. She pushed her coat away, pawed desperately through the bag, found the bill, uncrumpled it, and laid it on top of the other bills. Laura realized that she'd been hustled: Henry had been after her twenty all along.

He got a so-so break but still pocketed four balls. The cue ball was now frozen next to the three ball near a corner pocket. The angle was too severe to sink the three. Quick as a flash, Henry hit the far right edge of the cue ball, double-kissing the three into the pocket. It was a deliberate miscue. He smiled at her. She wondered if he knew that she had seen what he had done. But it didn't matter, she couldn't say anything anyway. He missed his next shot.

It was her turn. She was afraid to win, but if she lost, she wouldn't be able to pay for her cab. Her head was pounding, and then she was outside herself. She watched herself as though from above, she told Laura what to do, what to say, how excited to seem, how nervous. She made an easy kiss shot, then an off-the-rail carom shot, which was also easy, but looked difficult. She turned, with great deliberation, toward the muscular man in the T-shirt. "I never heard that expression C.P. Time before," she heard herself lying.

"No," he said impassively.

"But I can be so dumb. I remember, when I was young, I thought Billy Eckstine was white, because his name sounded," she made a quick adjustment, "sounded German."

"She say Billy Eckstine white, heh heh," the burly man announced to the room. "She say he German."

"What you know about Billy Eckstine?" the man with the blemish muttered.

She pocketed three balls in quick succession; one was easy, one was earned, one was lucky. "What time is it?" she asked the room.

"Time to change your life, heh heh."

She walked around the table twice, trying to decide which shot to take next. "Study long, you study wrong," the burly man counseled her.

She took his advice, shooting quickly, pocketing two more balls. Happy now, she aimed at the eight ball. Henry sneezed, trying to shark her, just as she was about to shoot. She aimed again, held her breath, and watched as the eight ball dropped beautifully into a pocket. She took the money.

"That's right," the burly man said protectively, forestalling any protest, as she had hoped he would.

Henry dropped back into the shadows of the room. Exhausted, she sat down at the bar and rubbed her temples. "Do you have any aspirin?" she asked the bartender. He didn't answer, moving to the opposite end of the bar, as if he wanted to get away from her. He turned off the radio and now she heard a clock ticking. She was getting a migraine. In the corners of her eyes she saw streaks of light, behind her the yellow light of the desk lamp burned with the phosphorescence of a flare, over the bar the silvered glass bulged and narrowed like a funhouse mirror. All she wanted to do was lie down in the dark.

To her surprise, the bartender set two aspirin and a glass of water in front of her. The water had a slice of lemon floating in it. "Thank you," she said. He didn't respond. He wouldn't even look at her.

Inside the cab, she realized she was shaking.

4.

She went to bed early to get rid of her headache and then woke up early to work on the article, a feature piece about the funeral and the Jarrett family. She wanted to write about two boys who might be dead because they looked too much like their cousin—about a cousin who feared his neighbors but not as much as he feared his imperious grandmother—about a grandmother who had lost a husband, a daughter, and two grandsons, but not her faith. There was too much to say, the story was too wide to fit, no matter how small she made her margins. In the end, she wrote only about Mrs. Easley, because Mrs. Easley was picturesque and because Laura ran out of time.

She handed in her piece before noon on Saturday. José Pereira and she were both working the weekend. "Not bad, sweetie," José said. He had made changes to nearly every paragraph, but it was as close to praise as she had ever heard from him.

"Don't call me sweetie."

"Whatever." He rolled a throat lozenge around in his mouth. "Another shooting, over at Cabrini Green. This could become your specialty." He handed her a small sheet of yellow paper. "Get me a reaction from the family."

Laura looked at the paper, studying his small, crabbed handwriting, which had once confused her. Now she could read it easily. He coughed, and she looked up, wondering if he was waiting for her response. He wasn't. He had already returned to his desk. "I know their reaction," she told him. "They're upset. I'm not calling."

"Do you want this job?"

She called the police and some neighbors, but she refused to call the family. Later she read the newspaper at her desk, which she had never dared to do before, afraid he would accuse her of shiftlessness. She washed her hands in the bathroom, because the ink had rubbed off on them. In the men's room next door, she heard José clearing his throat, and then the clink of his knife dropping into the basin of the sink.

She worked again on Sunday, but took a long lunch break, walking south into the Loop. The neighborhood was seedy but she wanted to walk. She passed beggars and homeless men and women, boarded-up bookstores, a Social Security office protected by bars. It was cold but the wind had died down; the sky was painted gray with clouds. Out of the corner of her eye she saw a black man approaching her. "Excuse me, do you have . . ." Before he could finish speaking, she was shaking her head forcefully—no, she wouldn't give him any money. She turned away from him. And then she realized what he had been saying.

". . . the time?"

She turned back, to answer or to apologize, but he looked at her with disbelief and revulsion and she couldn't speak. He was well dressed, wearing a suit and tie, probably on his way to a matinee at the Auditorium Theater or Orchestra Hall. He walked away.

She walked farther west, under and past the el, and then she heard someone calling after her. She ignored the sound, walking more quickly, but finally she turned. She saw a man trotting toward her. She forced herself to stand still and wait for him.

"I was calling you big-time," the man said. He was wearing a Black Hawks sweatshirt, but the shirt couldn't be warm enough for him. "I lost my wallet and I'm homeless. I need four dollar to stay at the shelter."

Overhead, on a mechanized billboard, a smiling blond woman raised a glass of juice up and down, up and down, saluting Chicago.

"I can't—"

"I'm hungry," the man said. "Three dollar," he bargained.

She gave him some change but he didn't leave.

"I know you don't like me. I know I'm just a nigger."

"No . . ." she gasped.

"Just a poor nigger needing something to eat," he persisted, sensing he had found her weakness. "You got enough to eat."

"Here," she said, opening her wallet and giving him a dollar.

"You said three dollar."

"No, I didn't."

"You did."

"Leave me alone." She walked away but he followed her. "Get away from me," she screamed at him.

He ran away. Laura blinked back tears. The whole world was stained and no matter how hard she rubbed, it would never come clean. *I'm not a racist,* she thought. *Tell them*, she begged the gray clouds, the dull sky.

KISS THIS BOOK

The book looked appetizing. The jacket design was impeccable and droll; the lines were forceful, spare, clean. The pages smelled fresh and clapped faintly as they were leafed. The book felt good to the touch.

Martha Willoughby was a widow, sixty-seven years old, quiet and stern. Sometimes she was lonely. And the book was very strong, the words were very powerful. She felt a twitch . . . down there. And the book was very sexy, her blood raced, her heart was in her throat, with one hand she caressed the pages, with one hand she caressed herself. The characters were very believable. (Especially the lawyers.) She could practically see and hear them—feel them—beside her. She rubbed the pages on her breasts, her nipples were tender, she became moist. She moved the book down, a little, then more, then all the way. The book was between her legs, and the book pulsed, the book throbbed, it was very lifelike. The book was wet, the spine was bent, her legs wrapped tightly around the book. She breathed more quickly. And he said. And she said. And I said, thought Martha. And quicker. And harder. And I said, thought Martha. And wetter. And I— and I—and I said . . . She sighed deeply. Then she withdrew the limp book and kissed it. And the book was still clean.

And Martha lent the book to a neighbor down the block, John Hartley, a mergers and acquisitions specialist, forty-two. Divorced, three daughters. And John didn't know how to meet people—girls. He didn't like bars—but he went. He liked to read. The book certainly looked good and, of course, came highly recommended. (Martha.) He read the book, still not expecting very much. Except—except it really was awfully enthralling. John stayed up all night; he couldn't put the book down. (But sometimes, sometimes he stopped and looked at the author's photograph.) And he missed his wife, in spite of everything. There was even a character like her in the book—Jennifer. And he missed sex, not only the sex, but afterward . . . And this one scene, Jesus, this one scene was incredible. And he grew hard, like a teenager, for God's sake. But this one scene. . . . And he touched himself. And grew harder. And he kept reading, he kept reading even as he touched himself. And circled himself. And moved up and down. And then he moved the book up and down. And then he entered the book. He was inside the book, his penis was enclosed by the book. "In you," John thought. "In you," he thought, as he rubbed. And as he thrust. And "In you," as he came. He wiped the book off. And the book was still clean.

And John lent the book to Laura Lerner, a financial reporter he'd met on a business trip in San Francisco, thirty, very smart. Single. She'd broken up with her boyfriend, who lived in Chicago. He didn't want to move, and she didn't want to move, so they had moved apart. . . . And she worked too hard: long hours in the field, too little sleep at home, always on the go. She hadn't been to the gym in, what, months. And she'd gained eight pounds. And she felt fat. And God, she was horny. But she didn't even have time for a boyfriend! Not until this deal went through, this merger she was covering. And she was tired, but she started reading the book anyway, maybe it would help her sleep. But sleep didn't come. And the more she read, the less tired she felt. Less tired, but more, well, *you* know. (It wasn't only the courtroom scenes that piqued her interest.) Call her a sap, but she wanted to be swept away like that, like Beatrice, in the book. Swept away, and swept into a man's arms (or a woman's . . . there was that one time in college), and just held. For once, she wanted someone to take care of her, to hold her. Someone like Jerome. Jerome, in the book, was tall and handsome and his hands were big, quite big, and his hands touched her (she touched herself), and he touched her lips (she touched her lips), and he licked her fingers (she sucked on her finger), and then his hands were beneath her, between her, in her. . . . And without even meaning to, she let the book creep between her legs, and she lay on her back, and she moved the book back and forth. She rocked herself and she rocked the book, and she put Patti Smith on her tape deck, and then she rocked some more. "Faster," she said, and she rocked faster, and "Faster," she said, and she rubbed the book faster and faster, and she came. And the book was still clean.

And Laura lent the book to her cousin Brian Hertz, twenty-six, gay. And Brian had broken up with his boyfriend, too. He found it hard to meet anyone. It was scary out there, people were sick. . . . And the book was a hoot, campy and charming. Paul, the helicopter pilot who saved Beatrice from the top of the Taj Mahal Hotel in Atlantic City, when the entire hotel was engulfed in flames and all the lawyers at the convention downstairs burned to death—he was very handsome. And had gray eyes. Brian had never seen gray eyes, but he wanted to. Brian didn't want to be alone. "Me too," he thought. He imagined himself inside the book, as one of the characters, talking to, sleeping with, Jerome and Paul. "Me too." And he put the book right up against his skin, he pushed and penetrated himself, oh yeah, the corner of the book was inside him. "Me too." And he came. And the book was still clean.

And Brian lent the book to Moira, she was taking a class

with him at the New School. Moira, twenty-three, had trouble reaching orgasm. But the scene where Jennifer masturbated . . . Moira touched herself. "Can I?" she wondered. And rubbed herself. And then touched herself with the book. "Can I?" She felt another twitch. And she was growing warm as she rubbed the book. And then her toes started getting warm. And flexing. And maybe one day she'd meet someone like Paul. And he would touch her like this. "Can I?" She was getting closer. I *can*, she thought. I can. Can. And she came. And the book was a little bent and a little moist. She dried the book with her blow dryer, drying each page in turn. And the book was still clean.

And Moira lent the book to her friend Cindy Arrow, but Cindy didn't have time to read it, so Cindy lent it to her brother, Terence. And Terry Arrow was a good kid, eighteen and a high school senior, but he was at that age when he didn't want to ask people for help, and he didn't want to be told what to do. What he wanted was to be treated like an adult. (Except, sometimes, when he still wanted to be treated like a child.) And there were words in the book the boy didn't understand—not the sex stuff, that he understood, he'd already made it with Sheila behind the Burger King. The words he didn't understand he looked up. And he really liked the whole environmental angle in the book, the recycling project, the suit about the toxic dumping . . . And the sex scenes—they were great! He had xeroxed some of the pages for the guys. He'd read the scenes three, four times by now, and they still got him hot. Even now, reading, he got hard (but he was always hard, his dick was practically raw, he jerked off so much), harder than when he fantasized. The book made it seem more real. Jennifer, the congresswoman who uncovered the whole scandal—he could feel her mouth on him. "Me," he said. And he put the book around his dick. And she was going down on him. "Down on *me*," he said. And the book went up and down, and Jennifer went up and down on him, she was taking it all in, she was taking in all of *him*—"Me," he said; "Me"—this was incredible, and then, too soon, he came on the book. He wiped the book off with a tissue, but he was still hot, and almost still hard, and there was still the whole strip poker scene in Part Two to read, so he jerked off again, and "Me" again, and came again, and wiped again. And the book was still clean.

And then, foolishly, Terry left the book right on the living-room floor, right next to the TV, where the baby could get to it. And his brother Walter, sixteen months old, a change-of-life baby, toddled in. And Walter found the book. And he gnawed on the book. He liked to bite. And he touched the book—he liked to touch. He liked to tear, so he tore out some pages (the scene where Beatrice was nominated to the Supreme Court after her impassioned defense of free speech). And he liked to pee, so he peed on the book. And he had to make doody, he liked to make doody, so he shat upon the book. And he touched his pee and his shit, and he spread them all over the book. And he turned the book over, and spread his pee and shit all over the author's photograph. And Walter's mother came into the room, and scooped him up, and gave him a bath, and put him to bed.

And the book was still clean.

ACKNOWLEDGMENTS

My thanks to Anita Addison, Amy Adelson, Ben Baglio, Billy Campbell, Paul Cirone, Dan Cohen, Janet Cohen, Janet Daily, Ernest Del, Colin Dickerman, Molly Friedrich, Peter Golden, Wendi Goldstein, Kelli C. Green, Kent Greene, Marti Greenwood, Jeanne Heifetz, Sheri Holman, Ted Johnson, Lincoln Kibbee, Ron Lux, Ghen Maynard, Larry Mizrahi, Leslie Moonves, F. J. Pratt, Andrew Richlin, Michael A. Ross, Carol Schlanger, Pat Sims, Cindy Spiegel, all the Steins, Brandon Stoddard, David Szanto, Rob Weisbach, and especially Geert De Turck.

A Note on the Type

The text of this book was set in Perpetua, designed by the British artist and social critic, Eric Gill (1882–1940), and cut by the Monotype Corporation.

Perpetua was the first typeface created by Gill and takes its name from the first book in which it was used, *The Passion of Perpetua & Felicity*, in 1928.

The roman characters are derived from stonecutting, for which Gill was known, and the italic face (originally named Felicity, cut 1930) is an inclined roman. Perpetua is widely respected for its light and elegant readability, and for what is considered the most distinguished inscriptional letters cut in this century.